──────────── ★ ────────────

It was colder than she had thought. She shivered and shoved her hands into her pockets. There were no stars in the sky. The only thing she could see were the gray-white wisps from her breath. Hill Street seemed so silent; but, she figured, it was probably always quiet at this hour.

To shield her face from the cold, she pulled her collar up as she quickened her pace. Hearing a car coming from behind her, she instinctively hugged the side of the sidewalk closer to the houses. She sensed, from the pattern of the car's headlights, that the car had slowed down. She began to walk faster and to look for a light in any of the houses. Seeing none, but hearing the car right behind her, she ran toward the next house's walkway and porch….

──────────── ★ ────────────

# MAZE IN BLUE

## Debra H. Goldstein

# W♦RLDWIDE®

TORONTO • NEW YORK • LONDON
AMSTERDAM • PARIS • SYDNEY • HAMBURG
STOCKHOLM • ATHENS • TOKYO • MILAN
MADRID • WARSAW • BUDAPEST • AUCKLAND

Recycling programs
for this product may
not exist in your area.

MAZE IN BLUE

A Worldwide Mystery/May 2014

First published by Chalet Publishers, LLC.

ISBN-13: 978-0-373-26897-9

Copyright © 2011 by Debra H. Goldstein

**Printed in U.S.A.**

In Memory of

Aaron Green

My father—who taught me to listen to the sound of words

Leo J. Pecher

who renewed my confidence in my ability to write

Judith F. Todd

who provided encouragement, friendship, and the solitude of her beach house for writing

# Acknowledgments

There is an African proverb that says "it takes a village to raise a child," and the same philosophy holds true for bringing *Maze in Blue* to publication.

Special thanks must be given for their time, comments, encouragement and generous support to Jennifer Goldstein, Stephanie and Brad Brooker, Stephen Goldstein, Mark Goldstein, Erica Green, Michelle Stern, Fran and Lee Godchaux, Teresa K. Thorne, Kay Kornmeier, Cathy and Leo Pecher, Carolyn Morgan, DeeDee Bruns, Mary Ann Smith-Janas, Patrik Henry Bass, Judy Todd, Nancy Borg-Miller, Dianne Mooney, William Winslett, Neeysa Biddle, Anne Strange, Joan Perry, Joy Collins and Joyce Norman.

My greatest appreciation, even though his blood runs Crimson, goes to my biggest supporter, my husband, Joel.

# ONE

*Sunday, December 5, 1971*

THE VOICE THAT woke Denney Silber had a quality of hysteria in it.

It was the voice, not the insistent knocking at her door, that caused her to open her eyes and try to get her bearings. The red numbers on her clock radio read 6:30. Was the sorority house on fire?

"Denney!" Ana called again.

Denney pulled the crook of her elbow over her eyes. "Do you know what time it is? Go away."

Still, the edge in Ana's voice compelled Denney to roll out of bed. Stumbling across the room, she pulled down the MICHIGAN t-shirt she had slept in.

"Coming. Ouch!"

She stubbed her toe on one of her boots and hopped on one foot to avoid the boot's mate lying in the pink shag carpet. Her head ached as though she had crammed something in there that wanted out. "Just a minute."

"Denney, it's important."

Denney opened the door to confront Ana, who stood in her terry robe looking like a waif, haphazard strands of hair escaping from her chestnut ponytail, clutching a folded newspaper. Without speaking, Ana offered Denney the paper.

"What is it?" Denney asked, unfolding the crisp Ann Arbor News.

"I'm so sorry," Ana said, following Denney across the room as Denney scanned the front page.

Denney sat down hard on her bed. Still foggy from too little sleep, she wasn't sure for a moment which article she was supposed to look at. The picture of Helen jumped out at her under the headline "UNIVERSITY OF MICHIGAN COED MURDERED." With a surreal sense of detachment, Denney read:

December 5, 1971: Helen Manchester, age 20, daughter of Peter and Cynthia Manchester, was found dead early this morning by two fellow students in the office of University of Michigan English department faculty member, Dr. Suzanne Harris. Ms. Manchester, a student research assistant

Denney's gaze drifted from the paper to the cream-colored leather boot that lay on the carpet. The tangled pile almost concealed the stain of blood on the boot's toe. During the night she had tucked what had happened into some dark corner of her mind, hoping to wake up to a time when Helen was still alive.

Yet, here she was, dead again—just as she had been when Denney found her.

Blinking to clear her tears, Denney skimmed the rest of the article, relieved and yet puzzled that her name was not mentioned.

Actually, the short article didn't say much. The first paragraph gave general information about Helen being found dead in Dr. Harris' office. The second part talked about her academic career, including her work as an organizer of the 1970 Black Action Movement food strike that supported having more minority students and faculty at the University.

Shaken, Denney looked up at Ana who stood nervously, knotting and unknotting her hands.

"Denney, I'm so sorry. Helen and you are—were such close friends, I thought you would want to know."

"I already knew." She pointed at the article. "Bill and I were the students who found her."

"What happened?"

Even to herself, Denney's voice sounded far away, as if she were down a corridor overhearing someone in a different room. "Helen was working overtime editing pages for the Middle English Dictionary. After our poetry class party, Bill and I went up to the English department to see if she needed a break. If we'd decided sooner. If we'd gotten there just a little earlier—"

"Oh, Denney, don't go there. It's not your fault."

Denney reached for a tissue. A tear escaped before she could use it, smearing the photo of Helen, beautiful and smiling. Helen's smile could always pull you into her orbit in spite of your best efforts. Oh God.

Needing a distraction, Denney's professional eye noted the article's placement and the picture's too-tight cropping. Someone had been too lazy to reset more than a corner of the front page. Then again, considering that it had been almost two before the police let them leave the English department, it was amazing that any of the story had even made the Sunday morning paper.

"You'd think the paper could have run a better picture of Helen than this four-year-old high school graduation shot," she said. "Somebody clipped it out of that freshman annual they sold us when we first came to U of M."

Ana sat on the bed beside Denney. "I can think of at least one picture the newspaper must have in its files. Remember when Helen spoke during the campus food strike when we were freshmen? My dorm had no food, and I had zero extra for a dart board."

Denney smiled. They weren't talking about pictures of Helen, but memories. "I remember. There also should be one from last term when the paper did that article about how dorm assistants smooth the way for new students."

Denney picked up the paper and read through the news story again. It covered the who, what, where and when, and touched on the why, but it didn't come close to capturing anything of the essence of Helen Manchester. Not her smile, her smooth brown skin, her integrity or her sharp wit. Not the way she hummed gospel music when she was focused intently on something or how she'd sometimes come up with insane ideas. Ideas like reselling store-bought doughnuts to double Mary Markley dormitory's homecoming float budget. Helen never kept anyone at arm's length. Her brilliance made everyone, including Denney, want to be a part of what she was doing, hoping a bit of it would rub off on them.

They had made quite a pair together. Denney was a short, plump New Yorker with frizzy brown hair and skin that burnt if anyone even mentioned the sun. In contrast, at five ten, Helen could be mistaken for a tall clone of a young Diana Ross, and she did a pretty good imitation of Diana at the Markley talent night, but her musical tastes ranged beyond Motown. She liked anything by the Beatles and had a special fondness for James Taylor and The Carpenters, randomly belting out "Fire and Rain" and "We've Only Just Begun," the two songs that stayed on the charts most of their freshman year. Her favorite, though, was gospel. "Denney," she often said, "there just is something special in the music of the Lord."

Gospel never did anything for Denney. She measured a song by its lyrics rather than beat, her preference being show tunes and country music. During the year she lived on the Hill in Markley, she regularly blasted the Wood-stock fish cheer into the courtyard.

Denney and Helen were never going to argue over musical tastes or worry about having to justify their "Doughnut Racket" to Markley's treasurer again. Helen was dead. Ana said it wasn't her fault, but if Denney had listened to Helen weeks ago, maybe Helen would still be alive.

They had opted to take Dr. Suzanne Harris' Poetry 331 class together to fulfill an English major requirement. The day Dr. Harris returned the first set of papers and nobody received a grade higher than C, Helen dropped the course. After class the day the next round of papers with low grades were handed back, Denney met Helen on the Diag, Michigan's central square.

"I just don't get it," Denney complained. "My paper was A/B quality."

"Take the class next term," Helen urged, rubbing her boot against the hard stone edge of the marble bench they shared. "Dr. Harris' grades are going to be low this time around."

"Don't be so dramatic. She's just trying to scare us." Denney hooked a thumb into the belt loop of her jeans. "The next grades have to be better."

Instead of responding, Helen glanced away. Her eyes darted around the Diag as if making sure no one could hear them.

"You're making me uncomfortable," Denney said.

"I'm telling you this because we're friends, but don't repeat it. Trust me, you need to drop the class while you can," Helen urged. "I know what I'm talking about."

"What are you talking about?"

"You remember my work study job iṣ as an English department research assistant?"

"Of course. You've been working for Professor Willoughby on that crazy Middle English Dictionary project for almost two years. How many times have you told me that Professor Willoughby is so slow that you doubt he will finish before we have daughters ready to enroll here?"

"Don't interrupt me," Helen said, looking around the Diag again. "Professor Willoughby doesn't care when I do my work, as long as I get it done. Usually, I'm in his office late in the evening when most everyone else is gone. The only other regular at that hour, except for a security guard making rounds, is Dr. Harris. She came by his office a few weeks ago to return a book he lent her and we talked a bit. It gets awfully quiet up there at night and well, Dr. Harris and I usually take a break together. Do you realize that this is the first time in the three years she's been at Michigan that she's had to teach anything except an honors seminar?"

"No, I didn't. So what?"

"The 'so what' is that until this term, her class load has been limited to two mini-seminars with a maximum of six to eight dedicated honors students. Now, she's teaching three classes of thirty, all taking the course because it is required."

"I'm missing something here," Denney said.

Helen gave her an impatient look. "Dr. Harris earned her degrees at Howard and Spelman."

Denney just stared at her.

"Two top historically Black schools. Her dissertation on the racial impact of poetry created a lot of excitement in academic circles when it was published. Not only was it excellent, but with the push for affirmative action, a lot of schools wooed her." Helen hooked a section of her long, black hair over her ear. "It was a big deal when she picked Michigan's offer over Harvard and some of the other Ivy League schools."

"I'm still not getting what you're trying to tell me."

Helen leaned closer to Denney, almost whispering. "The Poetry 331 kids not only are a shock to her system because of their disinterest in poetry, but because their papers are lousy compared to what she's used to getting from honors students. Add that to her own high standards and it's going to take a term or two for her expectations to reach our mediocre level—if she ever teaches mortals like us again. That's why you need to wait to take this course."

"I can't," Denney said. "If I drop it now and for some reason get shut out next term, I won't be able to graduate on time."

"Listen to me, Denney. I'm telling you as your friend that you need to drop Poetry 331." Without a doubt, Helen had been trying to act as a true friend. Something more than concern for her grades had motivated Helen and based upon Denney's encounters with Dr. Harris since that conversation, Denney knew she should have listened to her.

Taking one more look at Helen's picture, Denney handed the paper back to Ana and lay back on her bed. Lost in her own thoughts about Helen and friendship, she barely noticed Ana leave.

There was no question that Denney adhered to the give-and-take rules of friendship her mother had drilled into her head when she was a kid, but after being at Michigan, her definition of friendship had been refined. To Denney, a true friend was there when you had the proverbial bad hair day. A true friend dealt with your PMS moments and a friend was there when you broke up with your boyfriend (the mystery man Denney still was waiting to find).

Most importantly, friends didn't kill friends.

As strained as the relationship had been the past few weeks between herself and Dr. Harris, Denney doubted things were going to get much better now. She wasn't certain how the warnings Helen had tried to give her fit into the picture, but she was pretty sure Dr. Harris had broken the most important rule of friendship.

# TWO

*Monday, November 29, 1971*
*One week earlier*

DENNEY NORMALLY LOVED the long walk down South State Street between the Frieze Building and Mason Hall, but making the trek this morning in the scant ten minutes between her acting and poetry classes was proving difficult. An early dusting of snow hid patches of ice. Denney welcomed the concentration that every step in her new boots took, not wanting to think about the possibility of making another low grade in Dr. Harris' class.

She slipped into a seat beside Bill Smythe as Dr. Harris was handing out the class' most recent papers. Turning to look behind her, Denney counted only ten people still in the class since Helen dropped out.

Dr. Harris' hand appeared out of the corner of Denney's eye, placing a paper on her desk. A glaring red B- was scrawled prominently in the upper right hand corner. Her anger grew at the casual disdain the grade represented. She was an A student and she'd worked especially hard on that paper, trying to prove Helen wrong and meet the standards of Dr. "Honors Students Only" Harris.

She stole a glance at Bill's paper topped with a red D. Bill caught her eye and she blushed. "Your paper can't have been that bad!" she muttered under her breath, expanding her anger to include the wrong done to him, even though she had no clue what kind of work he'd put into it.

"Would you like to share that comment with the class, Ms. Silber?"

"No, I don't think I would," Denney replied before she could soften the sarcastic sound of her words. She forced herself not to look away from Dr. Harris' blazing stare. "It wasn't important," she added. "I really don't think anyone would be interested in what I said."

"Yes, we would." The instructor released the right side of the podium she had been tightly gripping and leaned forward. Her gaze was targeted at Denney.

Denney felt her face flame, but stubbornly remained silent.

Dr. Harris persisted in the battle of wills with eye contact, but began absently playing with the rubber band she had looped over her left wrist.

To distract herself from answering too quickly, Denney made herself analyze Dr. Harris' clothes. From the first week, she had concluded that what Dr. Harris wore to class was far more interesting than the way she taught Poetry 331. Today was no exception. From three-inch heels to a scarf expertly knotted to accentuate a designer suit and her coffee-colored skin, Dr. Harris obviously had considered every aspect of the final effect. Her carefully controlled look was a sharp contrast to Denney's haphazardly thrown on t-shirt and jeans. Even Harris' short, styled hair added to the fashion statement. Denney barely had taken time to brush her teeth and run a comb through her brown frizz before dashing to class.

"Well?" With one word, Dr. Harris pulled the trump of rank. If Denney didn't answer, she could be thrown out of class. If she said what she wanted to say—same result.

Denney sighed. She tried to make her voice sound more conversational. "I said I thought your grading system left something to be desired." Responding to hushed noises to her left, Denney stole a quick glance at Bill, slouched as low as his six-foot-four body could manage. She could not decide if the hand covering his face was being used to shield a look of mortification or hide a grin.

"What is not desired, Ms. Silber, is the poor quality of work this class has chosen to turn in." Dr. Harris now shifted her attention to the class in general. "If any of you would like to discuss your papers in more detail, I have office hours tomorrow and Wednesday between eight and nine. Now, please turn to page sixty-three of your text so we can discuss 'The Windhover' by Gerard Manley Hopkins." She paused to let the class find the page and then asked, "Mr. Hodges, would you please explain the formal structure of the poem?"

"I'm sorry, ma'am," Hodges said, possibly inspired by Denney's insurgency, "but I'm still trying to get over all the red marks on my paper." He held it aloft. "It looks like a road map." From different parts of the room suppressed snickers ignited others until laughter completely drowned out thoughts of 'The Windhover' or any other nineteenth century clerical poetry.

Dr. Harris stood frozen, again clutching the podium. Her voice, always cool, was now chipped ice. "It appears as if none of you can concentrate on anything except your grades today. I think it best we adjourn until tomorrow when perhaps you will be more inclined to give your attention to the job at hand. In fact, to make sure you're more into our studies, Mr. Hodges, you will present 'The Windhover,' while Ms. Silber," she glared at Denney, "be prepared to teach the class Shakespeare's 'Sonnet 18.'"

With the finality of firing the last shot, Dr. Harris shoved her prepared handouts back into her leather briefcase and left the room.

Denney threw her notebook and poetry text into the

bottom of her blue backpack. "I think I just blew my grade in this class."

Bill reached down to pull his worn green knapsack out from under his desk. "You think?"

"Did you see the look she gave me as she was leaving?"

"Don't worry about it," Bill smiled at her as they made their way out of the room. "It isn't every day that someone can stir things up enough to get a class canceled. I totally enjoyed it, and I really don't think you have to worry about your grade." He held the back door of Mason Hall open for her. "Dr. Harris may hate you, but she will be fair."

"You must know something about her that I don't." Denney slid under his arm and out the exit onto the Diag.

Before Bill could answer, a voice from behind them called, "Wait up!" Kellie O'Reilly jogged to catch up with them.

Like Denney, Kellie lived at the Collegiate Sorosis sorority house. Unlike Denney, who was an actual member, Kellie was a boarder. Since the University no longer required women under twenty-one to live on campus, many of the sorority houses took in boarders. Kellie had moved into Sorosis a few days after the school year began to fill its remaining spot. With her lively personality, quick wit, and athletic California looks, she was more of a throwback to the traditional member than Denney. Kellie and her roommate, Ana Martinez, were two of Denney's best friends.

"Are you going back to Sorosis?" Kellie asked as Denney carefully sidestepped the big brass M in the middle of the Diag. Michigan tradition was that stepping on the M before a freshman's first bluebook exam would result in flunking it, but Denney felt it safer to avoid the M until after graduation.

"No, I'm debating between going to the library to research whatever 'Sonnet 18' is or to the Ice Cream Shake for some sustenance." Denney ignored a student trying to press an anti-Vietnam flyer into their hands. "Unfortunately, I think the library is going to win because I can't teach 'Sonnet 18' until I know what it is."

Kellie waved a hand in dismissal. "That shouldn't be too hard to figure out. Dr. Harris clued you in that Shakespeare wrote it. All you have to do is get a copy, give us a few handouts, drone on a bit about the poem's structure, make an obscure reference to deeper meaning, and you'll be doing a perfect imitation of Dr. Harris."

"I don't think you should do it like that," Bill said. He ran a hand through his pale hair as he seemed to be searching for the right words. "You're funny. Instead of imitating Dr. Harris, why don't you just do it your way—informal, fun. It would drive her nuts."

Denney hesitated. "Well…"

"Bill's right," Kellie said with an excited laugh. "Even calling us by our first names would make the class feel more relaxed. The three of us can easily come up with the names of the few of us still in the class."

Bill nodded.

Kellie rubbed her arms briskly. "Why don't we go somewhere warm to brainstorm?"

"I'd love to," Bill said, looking at his watch, "but I have an appointment at the LS&A Building in a few minutes. Maybe we could get together tonight?"

"Are you meeting with the Dean or something?" Denney asked, avoiding his offer.

"The Dean and President Fleming."

She stared at him. "About?"

"Naming opportunities for donations to the University."

Denney bit back the smart retort she was about to utter. Bill's blue eyes were not gleaming as they would if he was pulling a fast one. He really was going to discuss naming opportunities with the Dean and President of the University. How could that be? Despite three years of being fairly active on campus, Denney had last exchanged pleasantries with those two at her freshman orientation.

Apparently oblivious to the skeptical look Denney knew was still on her face, Bill smiled. "Our meeting should only take an hour or so. I'm free the rest of the evening."

"Well, I'm not sure about tonight. I need some time to research this sonnet."

"Denney," Kellie said. "If you go to the library now, you'll have plenty of time to look it up before dinner."

Denney could not figure it out. She was being handed, albeit in a somewhat orchestrated manner, the opportunity to spend time with the cutest boy in the poetry class in a setting that wasn't a date she could blow, and she was fighting it. She again attempted to sidestep, but neither was giving up. Cornered, Denney swallowed and tried to sound cheerful. "Okay, I'd love your help. Dinner at Sorosis, the big white house on Washtenaw, at 5:30."

"No problem. That's the house almost at the intersection of Washtenaw and East University?"

"Right."

"I've always wondered how a non-Greek house got such a valuable piece of property on Greek row."

Denney was relieved to be back on familiar territory. "Sorority legend is that at the turn-of-the-century two sisters got mad at their Theta sorority sisters and had their father build them a bigger and better house directly

across the street. He also got them the only college char-
ter ever given by the New York Sorosis Club. The real
story is interesting, but not as much fun."

"I'd like to hear more," Bill said, "but I have to run.
See you both later."

Denney and Kellie watched him as he walked away.
"So," Kellie asked, as their view of him was obstructed
by other students on the Diag, "how do you rate his blue-
jeaned tush? Cute, isn't it?"

"Kellie! I don't know Bill well enough to rate any
part of him."

Kellie laughed at Denney's protest.

Denney felt her cheeks flaming for the third time in
less than an hour. "For that matter, did it ever dawn on
you that I might not want him or anyone to come over
tonight? I have a lot of work to do for my other classes."

"Me thinks you protest too much," Kellie teased. "If
this was Psych 101, I'd think you were trying to avoid
getting to know Bill better. Tell me," Kellie pantomimed
a psychiatrist taking notes while listening to a patient,
"why is this?"

Denney ignored her and began walking towards the
architectural nightmare of square and rectangular pan-
els that had earned the undergraduate library its permanent UGLi nickname.

Kellie quickly caught up. "Denney, seriously, with
Bill and me helping you, it won't take any time for you
to prepare for class and besides, you have to admit, he
is easy on the eyes."

The eighty-one bell chime of Baird Carillon announcing the hour provided the perfect excuse for Denney to
seize the moment to wave goodbye to Kellie and duck

into the UGLi. Hopefully, she could find enough information not to make a fool of herself in front of Bill tonight
or the entire class tomorrow.

# THREE

*Tuesday, November 30, 1971*

ON TUESDAY, RATHER than risk being late, Denney skipped her acting class to review the notes she had made at the UGLi. It had not taken long to find that "Sonnet 18" was the other name for Shakespeare's "Shall I Compare Thee to a Summer's Day?" The poem seemed pretty to Denney; however, she quickly realized pretty wasn't its deeper meaning. Recognizing deeper meaning was not a skill that came naturally to her, but she had learned to compensate with good research techniques. As this poem was an often quoted Shakespearian work, she easily had found a wealth of commentary perfect for cribbing lecture material.

Denney took a deep breath, made sure she had everything she needed, and headed for the classroom. Dr. Harris was not there, but Mr. Hodges already had staked out the chair closest to the door.

Kellie waved at Denney from the back row. A moment later, Bill passed Denney in the doorway, giving her shoulder a little pat before taking his customary third-row seat. Denney sat down next to him.

The Carillon had just chimed the hour when Dr. Harris entered. Rather than going to the podium, she took a seat in the last row of the classroom. The class waited in silence for her to make the next move.

"Mr. Hodges." She smiled at him, as he nearly dropped

his book getting to the lectern. He cleared his throat and began mumbling about "The Windhover." His monologue continued uninterrupted for ten minutes as the class stared at the sweat rings forming on his t-shirt. He finished, grabbed his materials and rushed back to his chair.

Not waiting to be summoned by Dr. Harris, Denney rose. She picked up her book and folder and willed herself to walk calmly to the front of the class. Denney stood still until she was sure all ten faces were looking at her. Without a word, she walked away from the lectern and began distributing a stack of rubber-banded papers. She quickly passed out her two handouts.

Instead of returning to the lectern, she sat on the first empty table. With a glance over her shoulder at the podium, she began, "I'm just not a lectern person. Please open your books to page three-hundred-ninety-two, but let's start with the handouts. One is a sonnet written by an unpublished writer while the second is a more traditional poem."

Denney mindlessly fingered the rubber band on her wrist as she lectured about the rhyming structure of a sonnet. Then, to emphasize the complexity of Shakespeare's poem, she called the students' attention to the unpublished poet's sonnet. "Bill, would you please read 'Doctor's Visit' out loud?"

Bill read the unpublished sonnet and looked at Denney.

"As you can see, this poet gets right to the point, hiding nothing. Shakespeare's sonnet is supposed to have more depth. One viewpoint considers it to be a comparison of a beautiful woman to a summer's day, while other scholars believe he is attempting to immortalize the virtues of a young man. What do you think, Kellie?"

Just as they had practiced last night, Kellie carefully

removed her horn-rimmed reading glasses and waved them in the air, reciting a textbook response supporting the belief that Shakespeare had written the sonnet about a young man.

When Kellie finished, Denney asked another member of the class to answer a fairly easy question. For the next fifteen minutes, she called, always by first name, on each student.

Denney then introduced the second handout poem. It dealt with war and was written in long verse. "Without using the word, this poem also addresses immortality." She looked to the back row where Dr. Harris seemed engrossed in reading the handouts.

"Suzanne, how would you contrast the two styles and the manner in which the poems discuss immortality? Is one more effective than the other?"

There was no response. "Suzanne?" Denney put a teacher's authority in her voice. "Suzanne, in the back row."

All eyes turned to Dr. Harris. "Me?"

"Yes, you." Denney grinned. "How would you contrast the two styles and the manner in which they discuss immortality?" Dr. Harris tensed, as if considering whether to end the teaching experiment, then visibly relaxed. With the hint of a smile, she delved into the subject, contrasting the two styles and then launched into a long discourse about immortality similar to the notes Denney had made from Dr. Harris' article on "Shakespeare and Immortality." As Dr. Harris finished speaking, the bell rang.

"Class dismissed," Denney yelled.

Mr. Hodges left the room quickly, but other classmates stopped to congratulate her and most agreed with Bill that an Ice Cream Shake celebration was in order.

Before she reached the door, Denney realized that Dr. Harris still was sitting in the back row absorbed in reading the handouts. Denney hesitated and then waved Bill and Kellie on. "Wait for me in the hall."

Not sure of her reception, but riding on the adrenaline of her presentation, Denney made her way to Dr. Harris.

"Would you like to join us?" she asked.

"Not today." Dr. Harris gave Denney a long look. "You did a good job."

"I found some good references to base my presentation on."

Dr. Harris pointed to the handouts. "Did you write these poems?"

Denney nodded.

"I don't understand how someone who can write poetry this well can't write better prose."

The backhanded compliment felt like a slap. Denney stood silently and then turned and walked out of the classroom to join her friends.

# FOUR

*Tuesday, November 30, 1971*

"YOU WERE WONDERFUL in there!"

"You showed Harris!"

"Think she'll have the guts to teach us again?"

Denney smiled, but concentrated on her menu as the gang filled most of the small tables at the Ice Cream Shake. Seated next to her, Bill asked, "What would you like?"

"Are you buying?"

"After that presentation, we all are," somebody yelled from the next table as students began to give the waitress their orders. In a few moments, each was too busy eating to give the class or even the next table another thought.

Savoring her one dip, Denney noticed her friend, Helen, in the take-out line. Denney knew from years of Ice Cream Shake evenings that Helen's bag held a double dip of Heavenly Hash ice cream topped with a dab of whipped cream and a cherry. Their differing metabolisms were the unfair cause of most of the Mutt and Jeff comparisons people made about them.

Denney had come to accept that whenever they were together on campus, all eyes looked first at her elegant copper-toned friend before amusingly taking in the little hop-skip-jump she used every few steps to match Helen's longer stride. From their expressions, she realized people often were surprised at their friendship. She never chose to enlighten them that Helen and she had bonded when, after being named co-chairmen of the Mary Markley Homecoming Float Committee, they creatively doubled their budget by investing Markley's float money in store-bought doughnuts that they resold on the Diag behind a sign that read "Buy a Doughnut for MMF."

Helen had comfortably looked people in the eye as she made them feel their doughnut purchase would help eradicate a horrible disease. Denney could only smile, say "Thank you," make change, and wonder what trouble she was going to get into after following her mother's advice to "get involved."

Since freshman year, their opposite strengths often complemented each other in campus activities. That didn't mean they didn't disagree.

Over the past weekend, they'd run into each other at the bookstore and stopped to have a quick cup of coffee at The Jugg. Helen again had tried to convince Denney to drop Poetry 331.

"Dr. Harris isn't warming up to her classes," Helen warned, taking a sip of her coffee. "I doubt things are going to improve this term."

"It can't get any worse. She has to lighten up."

"I don't think so."

After today, Denney was ready to admit Helen knew what she was talking about.

Catching Helen's eye, Denney waved for her to join them.

"This looks like the remains of Poetry 331," Helen observed as she worked her lithe figure around the table to stand beside Denney and Bill.

"It is," Bill answered as he pulled another chair up for Helen to squeeze between Kellie and him. "I know you were in our class for a few days and I've seen you up in

Professor Willoughby's office, but I don't think we've officially been introduced. I'm Bill Smythe."

"Helen Manchester. I thought I recognized you. I'm Willoughby's student research assistant."

"Oh, so you're the one working with him on the Middle English Dictionary."

Helen nodded.

"I didn't realize you and Denney knew each other," Bill said.

"Besides poetry class, Helen and I have been friends since we both lived in Markley," Denney said. "In fact," she added, looking at Kellie, "Helen is the reason I pledged Sorosis."

"Oh?"

"That's right. During our freshman year, Helen was an organizer of the campus food strike aimed at promoting more minority students and faculty members at Michigan. Because of the food strike, we dormies went around to a concocted sorority informal rush to get free meals. If it hadn't been for Helen, I probably never would have stepped foot inside Sorosis."

Food, one of Denney's best motivators, had gotten her through the door of Collegiate Sorosis, but once there, she fell in love with the nooks and crannies of the spacious old house, especially the library. She always found something new to read on its crowded shelves, but it was the carrying through of the sorority's pineapple theme in the wood trim carving of the bookcases, lamps and even sofa fabric that amused her. She liked the room's quirkiness, but more importantly, she found it the most peaceful place in the house. Denney spent most nights curled on the library couch in her worn chintz robe reading long after everyone else had gone to bed.

A side benefit of occupying the library's couch, at least

before everyone retired to their rooms, was overhearing choice bits of gossip as her sorority sisters and their dates talked softly in the adjoining living room. Sometimes, though, preferring to be in the middle of the action, Denney would sit at the white grand piano that filled a corner of the living room playing show tunes or cutting up with anyone who ventured by.

Helen's rich voice brought Denney back to the ice-cream parlor. "What Denney isn't telling you is that having the sororities feed everyone in the spirit of a mock rush was her idea, and it almost ruined our protest—not to mention our friendship. But we worked everything out."

"But I wasn't sure for awhile if we would," Denney admitted.

"Well, I'm glad you did. Why don't you sit down and eat your ice cream before it melts?" Bill pointed to the still empty chair.

"Thanks," Helen said, "but I have to get back to Willoughby's office. Proof pages came in today that he wants ready before some tenure-related deadline. Personally, I can't complain. Willoughby in overtime mode means a bigger paycheck for me this week."

"I didn't realize that Professor Willoughby is up for tenure this year," Denney said.

"Actually, there are four people being considered for tenure in the English department."

"Who else?" Kellie asked.

"Besides Willoughby, the other contenders are Brenda Henderson, who also is working on the Middle English Dictionary, Franklin Godbolt, who specializes in twentieth century English literature, and Dr. Harris."

"Harris?" Denney almost choked. "But she's hardly taught since she's been here!"

"The key is her scholarly publications," Bill explained. "She has published a number of things."

Denney knew that what Bill was saying made sense in terms of academia, but it irritated her that publishing won out over good teaching. She didn't doubt that Dr. Harris would be a shoo-in under publish or perish. After having found her article on immortality, Denney had taken a few minutes to find out what other articles Dr. Harris had published in anticipation of future writing assignments. There had been quite a few and at least one book attributed to her.

"That's right," Helen said. "Willoughby thinks she has a great shot for one of the two slots the big tenure committee is supposed to approve for the English department. He feels sure that she'll get tenure because it will be a feather in Michigan's cap."

"Since when did the great Willoughby take his head out of the Middle English Dictionary long enough to look at one of his fellow staff members?" Denney shook her head. "I thought he barely knew you were his student assistant."

To Denney, Willoughby was an eccentric assistant professor, who, by the fluke of luck of the original tenured professor dying, was now an important player in Michigan's development of the Middle English Dictionary. He had been enticed by his fellow Michigan alum, the English department chair, Dr. Ferguson, to leave some small school where he was teaching Chaucer classes, to take on the project. Although Sean Willoughby had lived and breathed the dictionary for the past few years, campus gossip claimed that except for the work his student assistant did, nothing much got accomplished. In fact, the rumor was that because Willoughby was so far behind the dictionary's projected timetable, Dr. Ferguson had hired Brenda Henderson, the original professor's student assistant, as a faculty instructor so she could concentrate her efforts on the second half of the alphabet.

"Very funny. Willoughby and I may not be bosom buddies, but he talks to me. That's more than he does anybody else, except Mrs. Henderson and Dr. Ferguson. He only talks to them because Ferguson chairs the English department and gets to recommend tenure while Mrs. Henderson works with him on the dictionary. Willoughby is absolutely convinced that Dr. Ferguson is going to recommend Dr. Harris and him for tenure."

Even if publish or perish was the key to getting recommended, Denney wondered if that would be enough to give Dr. Harris a leg up over the other candidates. A thought kept nagging at her, but as she tried to place it, she realized Helen was commenting on how she thought Suzanne Harris was nice. Denney was surprised at the change in Helen's feelings after the warnings she had given Denney on the Diag.

"You've become buddies," Denney accused. Ignoring the others at the table, Denney looked at Helen carefully. Helen never had the thrown-together look that Denney prized, but today, there was something slightly more upscale about the way she had accented her jeans and blouse. "Why, you're even wearing your scarf tied the way she does."

Helen seemed uncomfortable in light of Denney's scrutiny. She started to move away from the table with her ice cream bag in tow. "Remember, I told you that with Dr. Harris' office only two doors away from Willoughby's, the two of us usually take a late night break together."

"So, now you like her?" Denney asked.

"We have a lot in common." Helen clutched her ice

cream bag more tightly with one hand and pushed her hair back with the other. "Dr. Harris was raised by her mother and grandmother. My family is intact, but we both had to go after scholarships. The first scholarship we each earned was a $150 minority leadership award given by our local NCAA chapter. Obviously, we went to different schools, but we both earned undergraduate spending money by being English department research assistants and both became dormitory hall floor advisors in exchange for free room and board."

"You might have a lot in common, but you've been the one telling me to drop the course."

"Not because she's a bad person," Helen protested. "You need to drop the class because she isn't going to give high grades. Denney, you have to realize Michigan has been a big change for Suzanne. She hasn't made a lot of friends or even met too many people outside of the English department."

Maybe not, Denney thought, but Suzanne Harris apparently had the ability to turn on some Southern charm. After all, it was apparent that she had forged a deep connection with Helen in only a few weeks.

"Without friends or much teaching experience, how do you expect her to get recommended over the others for tenure? On the basis of her scarf tying expertise?"

Helen leaned over her empty chair so that her voice barely carried. "Look, tenure is a real procedural maze, but with her publishing and teaching all the freshman poetry classes this term, her credentials will look just fine." Before Denney could get words out of her already opening mouth, Helen continued. "It goes back to the offer Dr. Ferguson made to get her to pick Michigan."

"He was able to promise tenure in his offer?" Like all students on campus, Denney knew Dr. Ferguson. The

English department chair was one of the most powerful people on campus, but she didn't think he had that much power. A regular on the freshman orientation speakers panel, Dr. Ferguson, with his handlebar mustache, ever present bow tie, and deep-voiced assurance that "Not every student sitting here will graduate," unfailingly was remembered.

Denney bent closer to hear Helen whose voice had dropped to a whisper. Bill raised an eyebrow but said nothing. Kellie, who had been concentrating on her ice cream, sat straighter, obviously wanting to catch every word. Denney was glad the other students weren't in easy earshot.

"He couldn't promise tenure only because he recommends but doesn't select. What he *did* guarantee was extra research and writing time. She doesn't like classroom teaching, but she loves the college atmosphere for research and writing."

"So that's how she's been able to publish more than her contemporaries," Denney said.

"That's right. For the past two years he kept his promise by assigning her a very limited class load. She only had to teach two upper level honors mini-seminars per semester and then could use the extra class prep time for her own work. She's only teaching so many classes this term to balance her teaching load off against the other candidates."

"And that's allowed?" Kellie asked.

Bill nodded. "The selection committee fills the tenure slots based on the credentials provided and the recommendation of the recommending person. In this case, Dr. Ferguson will be making the recommendations for the English department."

Denney snorted. "So, all it takes is for the paperwork and publications to look right. Some system."

"Hey, I have an idea," Bill interrupted. "As a class, we've been enjoying getting to know each other at Dr. Harris' expense, but except for Helen, most of us haven't had a chance to spend time with her. Why don't we have a Poetry 331 party and invite her to come?" Denney sent him a daggered look. "We could get together at my place Saturday night."

"I doubt Dr. Harris will want to come," Denney said.

"Well, even if she doesn't come, we can have fun. If she does come, maybe she'll let her hair down and let us get to know her. Look, everybody," Bill called to the other tables, "Saturday night, my house. I'll provide a few things to nibble, and you feel free to bring dates, spouses, or whatever, so long as you bring your own booze."

"I'll bring some other refreshments," Kellie volunteered, as did another girl.

"Helen, you could bring Willoughby," Denney suggested.

"Great idea," Bill agreed, ignoring her not so subtle sarcasm. "I'll invite some of the other faculty members, too."

At the thought of bringing Willoughby, Helen laughed. "I'll try to come, but I've got to run now. See you guys later." She walked out, carrying her bag that now probably only contained half ice cream and half melted slush.

# FIVE

HELEN'S DEPARTURE SEEMED to be the signal for everyone to leave. Within minutes, the students disbanded in different directions. Bill fell into step with Kellie and Denney as the two walked towards Sorosis. When they reached the beginning of the redbrick walkway that wound its way to the white stucco sorority house, the three dawdled.

"It certainly is an inviting house," Bill observed. Kellie and Denney exchanged a look of unspoken agreement. This time they were not going to invite him in.

"Very much so," Kellie said. "We would love for you to come in, but Denney and I need to get ready for a specially called meeting tonight. Some of the girls are livid that for the first time since the Mudbowl's inception, Sorosis isn't invited to participate."

"Why is that such a big deal?" Bill asked. He glanced diagonally across the street to the open area they had just passed—the site of the infamous Mudbowl. The land, which was owned by Sigma Alpha Epsilon, dipped into a wide flat trench. Normally, the area served as the barrier between the Greek houses and the businesses on South University, but once a year, water was pumped into it to create a nasty mud puddle for the annual Mudbowl Challenge Football game. Empty, the Mudbowl looked more like a piece of real estate waiting to be sold than the site of a college tradition.

"To some of our members," Denney explained, "it is sacred for the Phi Delts and SAEs to play touch football in the mud while Sorosis and the Thetas are either the cheerleaders or take part in the great tug-of-war. One of our members, Marilyn Thompson, even traces her existence to the Mudbowl because her parents met there."

Bill laughed.

"To her, it isn't a laughing matter," Kellie said. "She's the one who has her friends so up in arms that our president called tonight's special meeting to try and calm things down."

"Neither of you looks very upset about not being included."

"I'm supposed to be Sorosis true, but the idea of muck doesn't do much for me. Even though I'd probably look divine in mud," Denney said, arching her head and extending her arm diva style, "I've always preferred to watch from the bank with a beer in my hand."

Bill laughed again. "Okay, ladies, I'll let you join the mud fight." His voice slipped into a self-pitying whine. "I'll just have to plan the poetry party all by my lonesome."

Once Denney and Kellie were inside the sorority house, they dissolved in laughter. "How could you do that?" asked Denney. "When did you become a member who has to attend the special meeting?"

"It was the first thing I could think of. Besides, he probably doesn't remember I'm a boarder and even if he does, he won't think anything is strange about me going to the meeting. What's important is that that guy really likes you."

"No way!"

"Oh yeah, why do you think quiet Bill decided to have a party?" Kellie sweetly inquired.

"He isn't quiet. We talk in class all the time."

"You talk in class with him all the time. Until the three of us started talking about you teaching the class, he really hadn't spoken to anyone but you. Do you know anything about him, other than the grades he has gotten on his papers?"

"I know he knows President Fleming."

"And that's about all you know. Let me show you something," Kellie said. She led the way into the library and switched on one of the two pineapple-based lamps in the room. "The other night while the two of you were working on questions, I used the freshman annuals to make sure we had the right first names. When I looked Bill up, I didn't find him."

"Maybe he is a transfer student like you."

"No. I didn't find him, but I found where he *should* be. Here, look," Kellie said, pulling a freshman annual from the shelf. She turned to the page where Bill's picture should be. It was marked "No Picture Available."

"So what? He probably isn't the only one who didn't submit a picture." Denney took the book from her and sat down on the patterned couch. She flipped to some of the other pages, but they all had pictures. "Maybe he just didn't have a high school graduation picture. That's what most of these look like."

"Well, I think it's curious," Kellie declared. "Maybe he's a serial killer and doesn't want to leave any trace of himself for the authorities. Or maybe, he's running away from something in his past."

"Then he wouldn't have let them put his name in the book, silly."

"No, he had no control over inclusion of his name, only his picture. Maybe W. R. Smythe is not his real name. After all, it is sort of inconspicuous."

"Inconspicuous if you spell it S-M-I-T-H, not S-M-Y-T-H-E. Come on, you're being ridiculous."

"Maybe, but you better know more about him before you go out with him," Kellie warned, reaching for the book and putting it back on the shelf.

Denney absentmindedly fingered the ribbed edge of a pillow on the couch. "I don't get it. First you push me to rate his tush, then to invite him to dinner and today you want me to check out his background. Not that it matters. He's shown more interest in the Mudbowl and Sorosis than he has in me. I think we can safely assume that he isn't going to ask me out so fast, especially after you and I just left him standing on the sidewalk."

"Oh, I think he'll be back. And don't say I didn't warn you," Kellie chided. At that, Denney threw the pineapple-print pillow at her friend and fled the library before Kellie could launch a return missile.

# SIX

*Wednesday, December 1, 1971*

"WHAT ARE YOU doing up so early? After last night's meeting, were you scheming so much you couldn't sleep?" Ana, Kellie's roommate, asked as she poked a fork into the ancient toaster. Carefully, she extricated a slightly charred piece of toast that had stuck to the coil.

From the kitchen sideboard, Denney selected one of the larger cups with a faded pineapple logo and poured herself some coffee. "Be careful," she warned Ana, placing her cup on the island where Ana was still tinkering with the old toaster.

Denney nodded towards the nearby butcher block table where Marilyn Thompson was reading the comics and spooning cereal into her mouth. Marilyn seemed to be over the scene she had made last night protesting Sorosis being excluded from the Mudbowl. This morning, though still in pink polka-dot pajamas and fuzzy pink slippers, she had applied makeup and fixed her hair. Denney wondered if Marilyn kept her hot rollers plugged in twenty-four-seven.

Denney frowned at Ana's fishing expedition inside the toaster. "I read that most accidents occur within a twenty-five mile radius of home."

"No problem," Ana replied inserting two more pieces of bread into the toaster. "I think they're talking about cars, not toasters. Besides, you know my real home is more than twenty-five miles from here." As the daughter of a career diplomat, Ana's home changed every few years. Her parents were currently in the last year of a posting to Germany.

They had met during her father's first assignment to the American Embassy in Spain, where her mother was working as a civilian translator. After their marriage, Ana's mother chose not to pursue her own career. She was satisfied to serve as her husband's hostess and diplomatic partner in whatever country he was posted. Although most of Ana's education was in American schools located in the various compounds where they lived, her parents spent a great deal of time making sure their only child became familiar with local customs and language. Consequently, Ana had a good understanding of the people and countries in which she had lived, as well as the ability to curse like a sailor in at least four languages.

"Did you come up with a plan to get even with the Phi Delts?" Ana spread peanut butter on a piece of toast. "Hands off!" She pretended to swipe at Denney's hand as Denney leaned forward to grab one of the two slices of bread popping up in the toaster.

Denney bit into the dry toast. "You know we agreed last night not to seek revenge. What would make you think that I'd even give it another thought?" Denney kept her eyes on the wall of stainless steel refrigerators and freezers that were behind Ana, ignoring the loud clink of Marilyn's spoon striking the table.

The meeting last night had been heated, but had calmed down after the Sorosis president shared a recent discussion she had had with Phi Delt president, Brian MacLaury, about the dumping of Sorosis. "To quote Brian, 'as a lot of the guys are dating Tri Delts, we thought our interests would be better served by inviting the Tri Delts to play in the Mudbowl.'"

Despite an undercurrent of grumbling from Marilyn and a few of her friends, the tension in the room dissipated after hearing Brian's explanation. Other than some humorous suggestions that Sorosis should get its revenge by seeding the Mudbowl with manure, the meeting adjourned so that most of the girls could get to the TV room in time to catch *Medical Center* with Chad Everett.

Propping herself on the island, Denney squinted at the product of Ana's breakfast productions. "What are you making? It looks disgusting."

"For your information, it's a peanut butter and banana sandwich. Want me to make you one?" Ana picked up the knife she had used to slice her banana and began spreading peanut butter on a second slice of toast. Denney took the other piece of bread from the toaster.

"No, thanks. I think you have to have an acquired taste for that kind of sandwich. Maybe that's what we should spread in the Mudbowl."

"Denney Silber, you better not do anything!" Marilyn shouted, forgetting that she really wasn't listening. "My mother told me that after last year's pledge prank, a lot of the alum are worried about the future of Collegiate Sorosis. Sorosis has always been so respected, but not now, thanks to your shenanigans."

"Marilyn, you might not have liked it, but a lot of us thought having frats send their pledges to Sorosis in the middle of the night to serenade our membership and then share a kegger was a brilliant pledge prank," Ana said. "It certainly beat tying doorknobs shut or Vaseline-ing and Saran-wrapping toilets."

"Not during mid-term week. Maybe that didn't matter

to Denney and you, but the alumni are sure it affected some of the girls' grades."

"Oh, please." Denney sipped her coffee. "Just because I had the idea to have my side of the house serenaded by the fish cheer instead of "Happy Birthday" and "Old McDonald" doesn't mean I'm going to come up with a Mudbowl revenge scheme. I don't have the allegiance to it that you do." Denney swallowed the last bite of her toast. "But if some of the actives want to do something, don't your parents board horses near campus?"

"Don't you dare ask them!"

"Relax, Marilyn," Ana said. "Denney's only kidding you. We all agreed last night that no one is going to do anything."

"That wouldn't stop Denney." She glared at Denney who was helping herself to one of two additional pieces of toast that had just popped up.

Denney ignored Marilyn. Turning to Ana she asked, "Is Kellie coming down to breakfast?"

"You definitely are up too early this morning. Did you forget that while you normally sleep until ten, Kellie has been serving breakfast at The Jugg for hours."

"Guess I was up too late last night. My mind isn't working yet." Denney yawned.

Ana spread peanut butter on the last piece of toast. As she began slicing the remainder of the banana she had used for her first sandwich, she glanced over to see if Marilyn still was listening. "I do hope Kellie gets a few hours off to go to the Mudbowl with us."

"You would think that she could find a better job," Marilyn said. "That restaurant is such a disgusting place. It must be so demeaning for her to be slopping what they pass as food when someone she knows comes in."

"I think the food is pretty good," Denney said.

"And I don't think working to get an education is demeaning," Ana added. "I envy her for knowing she wants an education so badly that she is willing to get up at 4:30 four mornings a week to work for it."

"I could probably pull off the manure prank easier than I could get up every morning," Denney said calmly. "Marilyn, you've raised this to a point of honor. The more I think about it, the more I think that the only way to continue the Sorosis tradition of being part of the Mudbowl would be to seed it. Are you sure your parents wouldn't want to help us get our revenge?"

"I don't think so!" Giving them a dirty look, Marilyn huffed out of the kitchen leaving her newspaper and dirty dishes on the table.

As Denney congratulated Ana on the success of pulling off the first part of their plan, Ana looked down at her hand. She had been gripping the knife so tightly it had left marks on her palm. "Marilyn gets me so mad by making everything seem so common and cheap. I shouldn't have said so much about Kellie, but Marilyn just gets to me."

"She gets to everyone. If she wasn't a legacy, she wouldn't be here. Ana, is Kellie really getting up that early four mornings a week?"

"Let's not talk about that. I promised my roommate that what she does is her business."

"Come on," Denney coaxed. She leaned forward on the island. "How can Kellie get up that early, do her assignments, and do everything she does around here? I'd be wiped out."

"She is. There are some nights she barely sleeps and other times she falls asleep still dressed, trying to study. I don't know how she can keep up the pace."

"How is it that none of us have realized how stretched she is?"

Ana screwed the peanut butter cover on the jar. "Because she's usually off and gone before any of us wake up." She picked up Marilyn's plates and put them into the sink. "When we are with her, she's always cheerful. She never lets any of us see behind the smiling facade. Sometimes though, in our room, she just can't hide how tired she is. I can't put my finger on it, but lately I think something more is bothering her."

"Like what?"

Ana rinsed the peanut butter off the knife and dried her hands on her jeans. "I walked into our room the other day when Kellie was on phone. She was pacing back and forth as far as the telephone cord would reach and didn't hear me come in, but I heard her say '...that isn't fair. My tuition is past due and that money is mine.' When she realized I was there, she ended the call quickly, but I know her voice well enough to know she was really mad and maybe a little scared."

"Did you talk to her about the call?"

"I tried, but she snapped at me. Then, as quickly as she got angry with me, she flashed me a grin and started kidding me about how eavesdroppers take everything out of context."

"Maybe you did?"

"I don't think so," Ana said. "I think she's in some kind of trouble."

"Then we've got to find out what kind of trouble she's in and help her." Looking at the clock on the wall, Denney jumped off her stool. "We'll have to do it later though, I've got to hurry or I'll miss Dr. Harris."

"You really are going to see her? I thought you only used that as the excuse to be at breakfast at the same time as Marilyn."

"I may believe that the only decent time to take classes

is between ten and two, with a lunch hour, but Dr. Harris doesn't. She insists on discussing our papers only during her scheduled office hours. I was too busy yesterday prepping for my presentation so I need to catch her today."

Denney started to walk out of the kitchen, but turned back to Ana, who was wiping the last crumbs from the counter. "It might be a good idea to make yourself scarce, too. By now, Marilyn has awakened half the house to tell them I'm going to dump crap into the Mudbowl."

# SEVEN

*Wednesday, December 1, 1971*

DENNEY RAN UP the stone stairs that led to the faculty offices rather than wait for one of the slow elevators. Near the end of one of the two hallways that housed the English department, Denney saw Dr. Harris twisting the key in her door. Jiggling the door latch and making a snorting noise, Dr. Harris did not notice Denney behind her. "Leaving early, Dr. Harris?"

Dr. Harris turned towards her abruptly. "Um, why yes, I was." She began fumbling in her pocket. Still clutching her briefcase she grabbed a wad of Kleenex from her coat pocket and held it to her nose as she let out a man-size sneeze.

"God bless you." Denney said automatically. "Sounds like you've got that flu bug that's been going around. I hear that unless you take care of yourself for two or three days, it can easily turn into something more serious, like pneumonia. You really should be home in bed, sipping tea and reading a good book."

"I was just leaving." Dr. Harris sniffled. "Were you coming to see me?"

"Yes. I want to discuss my papers in more detail before I turn in Monday's assignment."

"Oh," said Dr. Harris. "I really don't think today is a good day to do that. My office is so small." She pointed as if Denney had x-ray vision to peer through the wood

and pebbled Plexiglas door. Denney knew it was close
quarters. She had popped her head in the week before,
hoping to establish a face-to-face relationship. Dr. Harris
had been standing behind her desk plugging in a two cup
metal coffee pot that sat on the far end of her credenza.
On the left side of the credenza was a single 8 x 10 or-
nately framed picture of a slightly younger Dr. Harris
posed in her cap and gown with a serene older woman.
The woman was a dead ringer for Dr. Harris, except that
she was all smiles.

Hung neatly over the credenza was Dr. Harris' diplo-
mas. All other available wall space in the office was covered with books. Suzanne Harris obviously had brought
in more books than the university issued bookshelves
could hold. Even her desk had a small arrangement of
books framed with mock Chaucer bookends. The spines
of the real books were turned towards her side of the
desk, but the lettering on the bookends, which referenced
some Chaucer competition, faced the office's two plasti-
cized leather guest chairs.

Denney had lightly touched one of the bookends, debating whether to ask about them or the graduation picture. Dr. Harris' eying of her fingers on the bookend was
enough to make her remove her hand and talk about the
picture. "Your mother looks really happy in that picture."

"My sister," Dr. Harris corrected without further elaboration. She had then steered the conversation back to
the purpose of Denney's visit.

Today, as Dr. Harris sneezed again, Denney could see
that she really didn't look well. Her hair and makeup had
obviously been attended to, but her puffy eyes and irritated nose negated any effort she had made.

"I don't mind if your office is small."

"I'm sure I'm quite contagious," Dr. Harris continued,

ignoring what Denney had said. "You really shouldn't get too close to me." She turned to sneeze again. "I feel a bit feverish."

"I'm fairly hearty. And you did say we should talk to you before we turn our papers in on Monday if we hope to improve in your class."

"True, but I just don't think today is a good idea. I…" She sneezed again, without turning away. Denney took a step backwards.

"Honestly, you don't look at all well. Maybe you should extend the date to turn our papers in until next week so more of us can meet with you at the beginning of the week."

"That wouldn't be fair to the students who already have written their papers."

"Oh, that's no problem. Most of us haven't worked on our papers yet, and we can pass the word among ourselves at Bill's poetry party Saturday night. I know Bill invited you; so, if you feel better, you can tell everyone yourself. If not, Bill and I can pass the word for you."

"Ms. Silber, I don't feel like fighting with you now."

"I wouldn't think of fighting with you when you obviously feel so sick. Look, I'll be glad to tell everyone you extended the due date until we can talk."

"No, but I will promise to critique your paper in detail next week. Now, if you have nothing further to say, I think we should end this conversation, for the sake of *your* health," she added hoarsely.

She turned on her heel and walked swiftly down the hall.

"Bitch," Denney muttered.

# EIGHT

*Wednesday, December 1, 1971*

Disappointed by her unsuccessful attempt to meet with Dr. Harris, Denney peeked at Willoughby's door on the off-chance that Helen was working, but the office was dark. More frustrated and with hours to kill until class, Denney decided to go by The Jugg for a cup of coffee. Maybe, if it was slow, she would have the opportunity to talk to Kellie.

Pushing open the door of the restaurant, she looked around the room for Kellie's station. Pete, the owner, was pouring coffee for the one student seated at the counter. A waitress Denney didn't know was standing at the back booth taking an order from four boys. Closer to the front of the restaurant, a father, who had the flabby look of an athlete past his prime, and his young son were studying the wall of Rose Bowl pictures.

Denney sat down at the counter and pulled a laminated menu from an upright silver holder. As Pete placed a coffee cup in front of her, she looked towards the swinging kitchen door and asked him "Is Kellie in back?"

"Why don't you tell me where she is," he grumbled. "She didn't show up this morning, and she didn't call in."

"I'm sure she has a good reason."

"Doesn't matter now. See that sign," he said, pointing towards the front plate glass window. Even though the sign in the window was facing outward, she could read

'Help Wanted' backwards through the paper. "We got a policy here. You come to work or you call in. You don't do either one, you don't have a job."

"But Kellie needs this job."

"Don't matter. She knows the rules. What do you want to eat?" As Denney replied that coffee was all she wanted, the phone rang. Please let it be Kellie, Denney prayed; though, looking at Pete's face, she wasn't sure a belated call would appease him. From what Kellie had said in passing, Denney knew the job wasn't the greatest, but the convenience of being right around the corner from the sorority house and only two blocks from campus was the trade-off.

Pete was still on the phone. She couldn't tell from his face what the call was about, but she could see that he wasn't writing down an order. Hanging up, he took his rag and began wiping the counter area where the other student had been sitting. As he moved closer to her with his rag, he pointed over his shoulder to the phone on the wall. "That was your friend."

"Is she okay?"

"Said she woke up feeling sick this morning. Claims she lay back down for a few minutes and fell asleep until just now."

"So, she called you the minute she woke up…."

"But she didn't call on time. She knows the rules."

"She called you the minute she woke up! As good an employee as she has been, how can you fire her? You ought to give her another chance."

"I did," Pete said. "You want more coffee?"

Denney waved her hand over her cup. "No thanks." She placed two quarters on the counter. "I think I'll just run home and see if she needs anything. Should I tell her you hope she feels better?" Pete shrugged as he picked up the quarters and began wiping Denney's place.

Leaving The Jugg, Denney wondered how Ana had not realized Kellie had crawled back into bed. As small as their room was, a body in bed wasn't something you'd miss. The idea of going back to bed seemed inviting to Denney. Peaking at her watch, she realized she could probably squeeze in a good nap before lunch.

# NINE

*Wednesday, December 1, 1971*

DENNEY WOKE WITH a start, seemingly only moments after putting her head on her cartoon pillowcase. Kellie was standing in the doorway of her room. For a moment, Denney thought she was still dreaming as it appeared to be Kellie, but the Kellie before her was wearing Denney's favorite suit. The subtle gray plaid wool suit was Denney's standby for adult functions for which jeans just wouldn't do. Propping herself up on one elbow, Denney looked again. Kellie still was there in the suit. "What's going on? That suit looks familiar."

"It should. It's yours."

As Kellie took a step into the room, Denney sat up in the bed. She pulled her blanket closer. "I know that. I even remember lending it to you two months ago when you wanted to impress the parents of that guy from Boston you were dating. What was his name, Mike?" Denney looked towards her closed closet door. "But I thought you returned it."

"Tim. I did return it, but I had a meeting this morning and I had to have something conservative to wear. You know I don't own anything like this suit." Denney was beginning to understand why Ana had not seen Kellie when she flaked out of going to work. "Please don't get mad. You know I would have asked you, but you weren't in your room this morning when I needed something that would make me look dull."

"Gee, I think of it as a pretty sophisticated suit."

"Oh, it is. It's just that, you know, I'm more the sundress or low cleavage...."

"You carry this look well, too," Denney said, cutting her off, "but why did you need it today?"

Kellie took off the suit jacket. She held it in her hands, with one hand holding up the right sleeve. "I had to go to a meeting and I was in a rush after working this morning. I came down now to leave you a note telling you I have your suit, but that I need to take it to the cleaners because I got some perfume on the sleeve."

"Don't bother." Denney held out her hand for the suit jacket. "Why don't you just take the rest of the suit off and I'll get it cleaned?"

Kellie ignored Denney's outstretched hand. "No, I wore it, and I don't want to give it back to you with the scent of my perfume on it." She backed away from Denney's still outstretched hand. "Look, I'm sorry for not asking first. You know it had to be important or I would never have borrowed the suit without asking."

"And you know, I wouldn't have said no. Please, just leave the suit. I'd prefer to take care of it myself."

"Den, why don't we just pretend this one time that I asked and you said yes? Tell you what, I'll prostrate myself before you and beg," Kellie teased, bowing towards the ground. "Come on, let's go down to lunch," Kellie urged. Denney lay back down on the bed. Kellie hesitated before draping the jacket over the chair closest to the door. "I'll bring the skirt back after lunch."

Alone again, Denney decided she wasn't all that hungry.

# TEN

DENNEY CAREFULLY PLACED the spinach dip and the cake that Ana had helped her whip up that afternoon into a shopping bag, checking that nothing would leak during the long walk to Bill's house. She glanced towards the entryway to see if Kellie was waiting, but she wasn't. Denney thought she had heard Kellie's voice earlier upstairs, but when Denney had come downstairs, she had not seen her. She could hear voices and smell a sweet odor that wasn't entirely being blocked out by the burning of incense coming from the last room down the hall, but she doubted Kellie was with them. As a rule, Kellie steered clear of that activity.

Leaving her packed bag on the dining room's mirrored sideboard, Denney decided to see if Kellie was in the TV room. The room originally had been used as a courting parlor, but when the University became more liberal and men were allowed on the sleeping floors so long as the bedroom door remained cracked and three feet were on the ground, it was converted into a TV lounge. Today, the room was empty.

Denney decided to give Kellie five more minutes to show up before she left for the party without her. Bill probably didn't need much help until the guests started arriving, but Kellie and she had promised to come early. She didn't want him to think she had reneged.

Sitting at the dining room table, Denney absentmindedly gazed at the highly polished mahogany tables and matching chairs. Six nights a week, each chair was filled during dinner with young women who sang of raising their glasses high for dear old Sorosis before eating from mounded platters of food set out on the long wooden sideboard. White-jacketed busboys kept the food trays filled and cleaned up the dishes and kitchen, while the girls chatted noisily about whatever and whoever seemed important that day.

Except for Denney's bag, the sideboard was empty. Denney could see herself, as well as the other unused chairs and tables, in the wall-length mirror over the sideboard. Twice a year, the chairs and tables were removed by the busboys and the mirror reflected boxes of corsages on the sideboard waiting to be pinned on by nervous beaux who then twirled the sorority members around in dance. Over the years, the mirror had caught images of dancing couples who swore betrothals, some fulfilled; some broken by infidelity, family politics, or wars. Crew cuts, long hair, uniforms and tuxedos all had been reflected in that mirror, and yet the room remained the same. It probably would still be the same, Denney mused, if she ever had a daughter come to the University.

Maybe that's why the break in the tradition of Sorosis participating in the Mudbowl had been so unsettling. Even though she had no legacy ties like Marilyn, Denney liked the idea of continuity. In a sense, not being part of the Mudbowl made the full circle of things seem fragile, like Shakespeare's mortality. Whoa! Denney shook her head in astonishment. A moment where that sonnet actually made real sense!

The thought of poetry class startled Denney back to the present. She looked at her watch once more and realized she had been daydreaming for almost ten minutes. Her irritation with Kellie from the other day had dissipated, but now, it was building anew. Frustrated, Denney carefully picked up her shopping bag to leave. As she reached the front door, a breathless Kellie opened it. Her arms were filled with books, folders, and a large grocery bag. "Oh, good! You're still here! I was afraid you'd left without me."

"I almost did."

"Well, I'm glad you didn't. I never had time to make anything so I stopped at the store to pick up a few things."

"I'm sure they'll be appreciated," Denney observed. "I made the dip and cake we talked about."

"That's great. I thought you couldn't cook," Kellie kidded. "Oh, I'm sorry. I forgot I offered to help. Things got crazy and I had to go out, and—uh, oh, never mind. I'm really sorry."

"Don't worry about it. Ana rescued me."

"That's my roommate! I'm still sorry, though. Tell you what, let me just run upstairs and drop these things in my room, and then we'll go. Hopefully, we can still get there before everybody and make sure Bill has everything ready."

"I'm sure he does. And even if he doesn't, who cares?"

"You're right. Probably nobody would notice, but I worry about things like that. Growing up with brothers, I know guys can walk through a room without seeing their dirty socks and underwear on the floor. Cleaning up after them is a job I don't mind doing for a party, but that's one job I'm not eager to have on a regular basis." Kellie mockingly shuddered.

"I'm not worried about you. You'll either pick a guy who cleans up after himself or, better yet, hire someone else to do it," Denney teased. "Why don't you just put your books in my room instead of going all the way up to yours? You can pick them up later."

"Great idea. Be ready to go in a sec."

Kellie returned quickly. Gathering up their bags of goodies, the two left Sorosis and began walking down Washtenaw away from campus. As they approached the Hill Street intersection, the wind began to blow hard. Denney hunched her shoulders trying to make herself a smaller target for the cold blast. She wished she could put her leather-gloved hands deep into her pea jacket pockets but both hands were full.

"Too bad we didn't check if anyone could have picked us up."

Denney nodded but kept her teeth clinched.

"Look over there," Kellie said, stopping to point at a darkened house.

"I don't see anything," Denney said, giving the house a quick glance. She resumed walking, already anticipating the relief of putting the bags down in Bill's apartment.

"Over there. Look in that front window. Can you believe the size of that dog? I bet he scares off any prowlers."

Denney looked again and had to agree. Even from behind the glass, the large black Lab seemed to be sizing up whether they should be on his turf. Without thinking, Denney opened her mouth and let out a guttural sounding bark. As she barked, his ears perked up and the dog began to bark back. Denney pursed her lips and responded. The dog again seemed to make a conversational reply.

Kellie laughed. "Who would believe I'm going to a poetry party," Kellie said, "let alone walking there with a woman who talks to animals? Do you do this often?"

"No," Denney giggled. "Just every now and then. I've always been able to do a natural sounding dog bark."

"Natural sounding? I thought the dog had gotten out. Are you sure there isn't something you're not telling me?"

"Moi? Et tu?"

"Me? I have no secrets. I don't talk to animals or do anything like that."

"No secrets?" Denney inquired.

"Okay, one."

Denney leaned forward, inviting her friend to confide in her.

Shifting her bags from one hand to the other, Kellie quietly said: "I'm really scared that tonight's party is going to be deadly." Seeing Denney's crestfallen expression, Kellie threw back her head and laughed again, her blond hair cascading across her jacket. "Come on, there's Bill's place. Let's hope I'm wrong about tonight."

# ELEVEN

*Saturday, December 4, 1971*

KELLIE AND DENNEY carefully navigated the three ice covered stairs down to Bill's apartment. Located in an old house, the apartment was no more than a subdivided portion of the basement. A partial wall divider served as counter space for the corner designated as the kitchen, and as a break from the general living/dining area. Three doors in the far wall appeared to account for a closet, where Bill was hanging coats; a bathroom from which Mr. Hodges was exiting, drying his hands on his pants; and Bill's bedroom.

While Kellie added her bottles of vodka and Johnnie Walker Red to the mixture of soda, beer, and Gallo wine on the makeshift kitchen counter bar, Denney put her apple crunch cake next to some brownies on a small card table. The table provided Bill with an eating area that was distinct from the brown-ribbed sofa that faced a secondhand entertainment center.

She placed her spinach dip and chips next to a beige dip already sitting on the plank-and-cinderblock coffee table that stood in front of the couch. Professor Willoughby, looking every inch the preppy college professor in brown slacks, a tweed sports coat, and a green cashmere sweater, was pontificating from the couch to a few students. He picked up a chip and dipped it in her spinach dip. "Excellent," he announced, smacking his lips. Immediately, the students surrounding him began sampling Denney's dip. "Did you make this?" Professor Willoughby asked.

"Yes, sir."

"Quite good. Looks like your dip is going to get more action than Dr. Harris' offering." He reached for another chip.

"Is Dr. Harris here?" Denney asked looking around the small apartment.

"No, Smythe said she didn't quite feel up to staying after she dropped off her dip," he explained. "I haven't had you in class yet, young lady, but you look familiar."

"I'm Helen's friend, Denney Silber."

"Ah, yes. You've been up to the office a few times with Helen."

"That's right. I invited her to join us tonight, but I guess she couldn't make it."

"No rest for the weary," Willoughby said as he helped himself to more dip. At least two of the students nodded in agreement. "Your friend is very conscientious. Tonight, she's organizing some proof pages that just came in this afternoon. I'm going back later to do the final edit."

"Oh." Denney assumed he was going back to make sure his name was spelled correctly on the pages Helen had proofed. "Excuse me," she said pointing, "I need to get a bowl for his candy."

As more of the poetry class members and their assorted spouses and friends arrived, the small room quickly filled. Denney busied herself either helping Bill hang coats or replenishing the food table while Kellie, scotch in hand, welcomed guests at the door. Expertly, she showed everyone where to put their food or directed them towards the bar.

Hearing the door, Kellie turned and smiled at the

newest arrivals, but didn't make a move to welcome them. Denney stepped forward to ask Dr. Ferguson and Mrs. Henderson if she could take their coats. Kellie pointed towards the bar, but then moved on to welcome more guests. Without a word, Mrs. Henderson made a beeline in the direction Kellie had indicated, but Dr. Ferguson remained facing Kellie, ignoring Denney.

Uncertain as to what to do, but figuring Kellie could handle herself, Denney, laden with coats, turned away. Bill relieved her of her load. As he took the coats, he thanked her again for coming and helping with the hosting duties. "I haven't done anything except pick up a little bit and that was only after I saw someone trying to hide a chip covered with that beige dip in one of your bookshelves," Denney protested. She retrieved a coat from Bill and hung it on the last hangar in his closet. "Speaking of that dip, I understand Dr. Harris still isn't feeling well?"

"I think she's okay, but I don't think she felt comfortable staying tonight."

"I understand that. What with the way most of us feel about her," Denney said as Bill and she checked out the food table. Although there were now cookies, nuts, and a cake, Denney's chocoholic gene immediately drew her to the plate of fudge brownies. Selecting one with nuts, she bit in and was so absorbed she almost didn't hear Bill's response.

"No. You two got into it, but most of us could care less. We come to class, try to stay awake, and are willing to take whatever grade we receive as our passage out."

Denney didn't bristle. Instead she took another bite and swallowed before saying, "I still think she's something that rhymes with witch, but you're right. I'm the only one who feels that way. Apparently, Helen, Willoughby, and even you have seen a different side of her."

"We've had more of an opportunity to get to know her." Bill tilted his head back to pop a handful of nuts into his mouth.

"I'll pass on building that friendship, thanks. I may be influenced by my grades, but I definitely think she has a nasty side that she doesn't show all the time." Slipping her hand down near the slightly bulging waistline of her jeans, Denney decided not to have a second brownie. "Let's face it, if she didn't have a hard edge, she couldn't have moved ahead like she's done."

"You're making her sound ruthless again."

"Not really. Dr. Harris is in a field where advancement is still harder for a woman, let alone a black one. The give and take is just part of getting promoted. When we were freshmen, did you have that assistant professor in the English department who was so popular but didn't get tenure?"

"You mean Forsythe?"

"Yeah, that's the one. A few years ago, U of M gave Willoughby's predecessor tenure for his work on the Middle English Dictionary, even though nobody was thrilled to take any of his classes, but Forsythe, who could really teach, they denied tenure. He probably was one of the most gifted teachers Michigan ever had, but because he didn't publish much, they wouldn't give him tenure. One of the girls on my hall got up a petition trying to keep him, but Dr. Ferguson ignored it. He told her everybody isn't Michigan material and that there are other things more valuable than just his teaching that have to be considered in the maze of making tenure decisions. Forsythe and his wife having a new baby or students loving his classes wasn't a part of the departmental equation."

Bill nodded. "I think I better go help Kellie," he said,

grabbing a last handful of nuts. "Looks like Dr. Ferguson has her cornered in the dining room."

Amused at Bill's description of the card table area, Denney had to agree with Bill that Kellie looked like a trapped animal. Why was Dr. Ferguson, the powerful chairman of the English department, standing so close to her? Even from where she was, Denney could see the contrast of the seriousness on his face and the comic relief of his bow tie bobbing over his Adam's apple. Whatever he was saying did not appear to please Kellie much.

"Ah, the white knight has arrived," Mrs. Henderson said, coming up behind Denney.

Startled, Denney jumped slightly. "Mrs. Henderson, you scared me. It's nice to see you again." She noted that Mrs. Henderson looked dressed for an evening that included more than a student party. Except for earrings and a watch, Mrs. Henderson was not wearing any jewelry, but her outfit was set off with a blue scarf, the exact shade of her eyes, tied in the same way that Helen had learned from Dr. Harris.

Sipping her drink, Mrs. Henderson's eyes remained on the group as Bill broke up the serious discussion going on between Kellie and Ferguson. "What a shame. That looked like it was going to be interesting." She drained her drink and walked off to pour a refill.

Mouthing a farewell to Mrs. Henderson's back, Denney turned her attention back towards Kellie and Dr. Ferguson, but neither was in the room. Looking around, she saw that the third door was now slightly ajar. No, thought Denney, what was Kellie thinking? Denney started across the room to rescue Kellie, but then thought better of it. Instead, she sat down on the floor near the couch and tried to concentrate on a somewhat heated discussion between Professor Willoughby and Mr. Hodges. From the sound of the difference in their opinions, she gathered it would be wise for Hodges to never take a class from Professor Willoughby.

At ten, as if the class dismissal bell had rung, the room emptied with a flurry of goodbyes. Dr. Willoughby walked across the room towards Mrs. Henderson. "Brenda," he said politely, "may I see you home?" Not getting a response, he asked, "Do you have a coat?" Apparently missing Mrs. Henderson's slight nod, he continued. "He's not coming back tonight."

"I know. The prick."

# TWELVE

*Saturday, December 4, 1971*

TEN MINUTES AFTER Professor Willoughby and Mrs. Henderson left, Bill, Denney, Mr. Hodges and a student Denney didn't know, were the only ones still in the apartment. Denney began to pick up napkins and glasses. "Leave them," Bill said. "I'll clean up later."

"Yes, do clean up later," Mr. Hodges said. He pulled a small plastic bag out of his pocket. "I brought a little something so we can have our own poetry party."

"Great!" The other student plopped down on the couch. The two waited for Bill and Denney to join them.

"Count me out," Denney said. "You guys go ahead. I'll finish cleaning up." She reached for the plastic glass Bill had in his hand.

"Tell you what," Bill told Denney, "give me a minute with these guys, then I'll take you home."

"That's okay, Bill."

"No, at this hour, I'd feel better not having you walk home alone." He went over to Mr. Hodges and put an arm around his shoulders. "My landlord is pretty particular about no smoking of anything in this house. Why don't we all go out back?" Bill guided him towards the slightly open third followed after taking the last chip that lay on the plate near the remains of Denney's dip. "I may not have the biggest apartment in Ann Arbor, but it does offer the opportunity to entertain on both the front and the back steps." Bill let them go through the doorway first before following them up the cement steps that led to the backyard.

"If that goes outside, where do you sleep?" Denney asked.

"I didn't know you cared," Bill said, signaling the other two to go ahead as he came back into the kitchen. "You've actually been leaning against my bed most of the evening." He pointed to the sofa. "It pulls out, but it really is quite comfortable. I can show you how it works when I get back." Denney wasn't sure if he was leering at her or just pulling her leg.

Once the boys left, Denney began tidying the apartment. She threw Dr. Harris' dip into the grocery bag Kellie had brought. She quickly added the few cups and napkins scattered throughout the apartment and then tossed the empty Johnnie Walker Red bottle, as well as the soda and beer cans from the bar, into her garbage bag. Uncertain whether to take the partially filled bottle of vodka back to Kellie, she opted to leave it on the kitchen counter.

Making a cursory final check to be sure there was nothing in the room she had missed, she decided she was done. She didn't know how long Bill would be. It seemed stupid to wait for him because by the time he got back, if he remembered to come back, she could be home. Retrieving her jacket, Denney let herself out through the front door. Unable to lock it, she made sure it was pulled tight. She stopped for a moment on the stairs to zip her jacket.

It was colder than she had thought. She shivered and shoved her hands into her pockets. There were no stars in the sky. The only thing she could see were the gray-white wisps from her breath. Hill Street seemed so silent; but, she figured, it was probably always quiet at this hour.

As Denney walked past the house where her dog friend had barked from the window, she looked for him, but curtains now blocked her view. To shield her face from the cold, she pulled her collar up as she quickened her pace. Hearing a car coming from behind her, she instinctively hugged the side of the sidewalk closer to the houses. She sensed, from the pattern of the car's headlights, that the car had slowed down. She began to walk faster and to look for a light in any of the houses. Seeing none, but hearing the car right behind her, she ran towards the next house's walkway and porch, hoping someone would answer the doorbell quickly.

# THIRTEEN

*Saturday, December 4, 1971*

"DENNEY! DENNEY," Bill called. "Get in. You've got to be freezing! Where are you going?" he yelled as she began running up the walkway.

Denney stopped abruptly and turned around.

Bill was leaning across the seat of a dark green Ford Mustang towards the open window on the passenger's side. "Come on. Get in," he repeated.

She didn't move. "I didn't know you had a car."

He gestured with his hand, but said nothing. "What happened to the guys?" she asked.

"I convinced them they'd be warmer and happier back at Hodges' place than in the backyard, so I got them to agree to let me give them a ride home. When I got back, you had already left." As Denney made no move to get into the car, he explained that since his landlady didn't have a car, she let him park in her empty garage. In exchange, he took her to the grocery store once a week.

"How did you find such a deal so close to campus?"

"Look, before you freeze, get in, and I'll tell you the whole story," Bill urged. "It really isn't that complicated. My mom and my landlady were best friends when they were students here years ago. They stayed in touch and, well, actually, my landlady also is my godmother. So when I was starting to look for a place to live this year, mom mentioned it to Aunt Maisie. Her basement apartment tenant just happened to be graduating and, as they say, the rest is history." Bill slid back behind the wheel, as Denney finally opened the car door.

"Isn't it funny living with your godmother?" Denney asked as she got in.

"Not really. Other than the grocery store run and occasionally inviting me for a free home cooked meal, she gives me privacy. I guess the only other difference is that Mom can call Aunt Maisie as often as she wants to be reassured everything is okay."

Bill put the car back into gear, looked to see if the street was clear, and pulled away from the curb. "Mom also feels we're doing a good deed by my living here. Aunt Maisie went through a pretty rough divorce a few years ago. Unlike my mom, who believes whether you're married or not, you're responsible for yourself, Aunt Maisie was totally dependent on her husband."

Denney made a face in disbelief.

"That's why the garage was empty," Bill said. "He took their car."

"She could have gotten another one."

"Believe it or not, she hasn't driven since she was a teenager. Over the years, she never renewed her license."

"Sounds like a strange lady," she said, interested in Bill's story.

Bill stopped for the Hill and Washtenaw traffic light and looked to his left to see what color the big rock that sat on the corner was painted. Although it was prohibited to desecrate the rock, it somehow managed to receive a colorful paint job every few weeks. Tonight it was a pretty shade of blue. "Basically, Aunt Maisie was so busy being a perfect faculty wife that she never really developed her own identity. Once they got divorced, she found a lot of their faculty friends were fickle. They

stayed with him because of his position on staff, and she
found herself lost."

"And now?" Denney demanded.

"Now what?" he asked as he turned onto Washtenaw.

"What happened to your landlady? She sounds like
a classic case of an abused wife. Is she getting counsel-
ing? She sounds so depressed." Denney turned so she
could face Bill.

"Anything but. Driving still isn't her thing, but she's
got a job she can walk to selling giftware at that department store on State Street. They like her because she's a
reliable older woman who has a knack for making cus-
tomers happy. In fact, after she worked there about six
months, the department manager quit and they promoted
her to department manager. You've probably seen her
in the giftware department." He paused as he crossed
through an intersection. "Between her work friends and
doing volunteer work with the UM Little Theatre Group,
she's busy and happy."

"Anything bad happen to that husband of hers?"

"No. You saw him tonight."

"Excuse me?"

"Ferguson. She and Dr. Ferguson were married for
twenty years. He probably was faithful for about half
of that," Bill said, slowing down to let the car in front
of him turn.

"So, that's how you got Dr. Ferguson to show up.
You're his godson!" Denney was incredulous that Dr.
Ferguson had been brazen enough to come to his old
home when there was a possible chance of running into
his ex-wife. To think that he had left the party with Kellie seemed even more insulting.

"He's not my godfather. Dad adored Aunt Maisie and
agreed with Mom that she should be my godmother, but

he was adamant that Dr. Ferguson couldn't be my godfather. Mom says it was one of the most major disagree-
ments they ever had because he wouldn't tell her why.
He would only say that he had done some things in the
past that Dad didn't approve of. One of Dad's other frat
brothers is my godfather."

"Your Dad and Ferguson were frat brothers?" Denney sat back in her seat as Bill, approaching the Sorosis
driveway, turned on his blinker.

"Oh no, Dad is much younger. By the time Dad was
a Phi Delt, Ferguson was the faculty advisor. He still is
for that matter. He claims it helps to keep him young and
connected to the students. Personally, I think it may keep
him connected, but I don't ever remember him being
young."

"Are you a Phi Delt, too?"

"Legacy, no less. I just don't live in," Bill said, turning into the driveway. "Last year was enough for me. Between keggers, football games, and Mudbowl activities,
I had a hard time sticking to my studies. My parents and
I agreed it would be better for me to live out this year."

"New subject," Denney said as Bill pulled into the
long driveway. "How come the Phi Delts left Sorosis out
of the Mudbowl this year?"

"Because nobody knew you guys."

"You know me." Denney pushed her face towards Bill.
Braking, he put his hands up in mock protest.

"Now I do, but not when the decision was made. If I
had known you, I would have gone to the mat for Sorosis." He grinned. "Look, to be honest, most of us could
care less about the Mudbowl so when the discussion of
dropping Sorosis came up, we deferred to those who had
the loudest voices because they were willing to work
on it."

"Well, somebody had to campaign to break tradition."

"You give us too much credit. Our meetings are not real organized. When you talk about tradition, the reality is that tradition at the Phi Delt house is whatever happened five minutes ago."

"I doubt that." Denney unlocked the car door.

"No, really, the decision was based upon the fact that three guys are dating Tri Delts and no one is dating anyone from Sorosis. Compare it to this—you asked me why so many of the faculty came tonight. The answer is easy, I invited them and they came."

"Somehow, I don't think they would have come for me. There's something missing here," Denney said, staring at Bill.

"Nothing is missing. When I came to visit in the summers, I would hang out a bit in the English department. Actually, I would run up and down the halls annoying people." Bill laughed. "Ask your friend Helen. Since she spends so many hours working up there, she has to have gotten to know a lot of the faculty, too. She'll tell you, everyone has a story, but basically they all are neurotic normal people."

"That's a bit trite."

"And I thought I sounded profound."

"Speaking of Helen," Denney said, "I wonder if Willoughby ever made it back after he took Mrs. Henderson home?"

"I'm sure he did." Denney opened the car door, which creaked as if in need of oiling. "If you want," Bill said, "we can go check on her. If she's still working, we can rescue her and the three of us can get something to eat?"

Pointing to the car's clock, Denney said: "I'm game, but I'm sure the building is locked."

"Not a problem. From the beginning of time, there

always has been a way into any building on campus—
even if you have to use the maze of steam tunnels that
run under all of the buildings. Trust me."

"Okay," she said somewhat dubiously. "I'm sure if
Helen is still there, she could use a break." Getting back
in, she slammed the car door shut.

Bill put the Mustang in gear and looped the circle that
led back to the street. As he carefully merged back onto
Washtenaw, Denney wondered what it must have been
like to have young Billy running and jumping through
the staid faculty office area. The image of him tweaking
Dr. Ferguson's bow tie made her giggle, though she really couldn't imagine Ferguson interacting with a child.

As they reached the main intersection of Washtenaw
and East University, Bill went straight and got on Geddes. Leaning over, but watching the road, he pushed sev-
eral buttons on the radio until he finally selected a station
playing what Denney would definitely classify as Musak
mood music. Softly, he began humming to the music.
Occasionally, his eyes left the road, and he turned to give
Denney a shy smile.

A block down Geddes, across from a small cemetery
that had been one of the first settler cemeteries, but was
now landlocked by university development, they stopped
for a red light. For years, students had regularly scaled
the cemetery's fence to hold picnics, séances, or whatever amidst those quietly resting there; however, the year
before Denney had come to the University, the body of
one of the first woman law students to live on campus
had been found in the cemetery during spring break.
The police had questioned everyone in the law school
dorm, but the most they had learned was that somebody
thought they remembered seeing her riding on the back
of a motorcycle. This alleged sighting, coupled with the

fact that she previously had shared rides with people who posted on the law school ride board, led the police to believe she had chosen the wrong way to go home for vacation. Despite an intensive investigation, the police failed to make an arrest in the case. Between the murder and other seemingly unrelated campus incidents, campus security had been significantly tightened by the time Denney arrived on campus. Escort services and a campus-wide shuttle now existed to make sure coeds didn't have to walk anywhere without protection.

Pointing to his right Bill asked, "Have you ever visited the cemetery?"

"No, and I don't think I want to start now." Or ever, thought Denney. "Didn't you miss the turn to the Diag?"

"Oh, you mean South University? Not really, this street is a little longer because it winds by the hospital entrance, but it has more side streets off of it where we can find parking closer to the Diag."

As the light changed and Bill drove towards the hospital, Denney felt relieved. Glancing at Bill, she doubted that he was a serial killer. Faculty members obviously liked him, but then again wasn't the murderer in every book she read a person who people usually liked or sympathized with? A person who was around so often that their presence was thought to be commonplace? A person whose picture might not appear next to his name in the freshman annual?

Denney looked at Bill and wondered what she was doing riding around in the middle of the night with somebody she hardly knew. She calculated how long it would take her friends to find her, or for that matter to look for her. Thinking it through, she decided she probably was safe because if she came up missing, everything would point to Bill. At least Kellie and Ana knew she had gone to a party at his house, and both Hodges and his friend would remember—maybe—that they had left before she did.

"I think this is the best we're going to be able to do," Bill said as he pulled into a parking spot. Getting her bearings, Denney realized, as Bill came around the car to open her door, that they were about a half block from the Diag. Giving Denney his hand, he helped her out of the car. As they walked, heads bent against the gusting wind, Denney wondered how anyone could really like Ann Arbor winters. To her, even with the overabundance of white snow that stuck to the grass, Ann Arbor winters were gray and dismal. It was a point she often disputed with Helen.

No matter what argument she made, Helen would laugh. She loved Ann Arbor winters. Often, late at night, she would take a tray borrowed from the Markley dining room and go to the Arboretum with her friends to "tray" down hills covered with snow and sheets of ice. During the days, while Denney was chilled by the wind that was caught and bounced back from the buildings as the two walked across campus, Helen relished the crisp coldness laced with escaping steam from the underground tunnels.

Bill interrupted her thoughts. "What are you thinking about?"

Thinking it was wiser not to share her real thoughts about serial killers or the differences she and Helen had about winter, Denney replied, "I was wondering how anybody can have the Middle English Dictionary as the primary focus of their life. I was thinking of Willoughby, and wondering what he has beyond A to Z."

"He doesn't even have that much."

"Pardon?"

"Willoughby only is working on A to M."

"For all these years?"

"That's right. His efforts have gotten hung up on A to M. That's why Ferguson brought Brenda Henderson on board as an instructor. She was familiar with the dictionary from her work as a student assistant so he felt she could concentrate on the remainder of the alphabet. Apparently, her presence hasn't helped much, because Ferguson has begun setting deadlines for them and hinting that if they don't speed up, he may have to rearrange the Middle English Dictionary staffing after the tenure decisions are made. That's why Helen had to work tonight instead of coming to our party."

"I thought the rush was over some proofs."

"It is, but Dr. Ferguson arbitrarily set the deadline."

"Sounds like between funding, teaching assignments, tenure recommendations, and whatever, he's a tyrant."

"You might say that. He'd say he just is doing his job to make the English department run smoothly and be recognized for its scholarly achievements. And to be honest," Bill continued, "he has advanced the image of the English department by sticking to publish or perish and replacing those who don't with faculty members who can advance his national goals."

"Like Dr. Harris?"

"Exactly. While her hiring immediately helped in terms of affirmative action, she rapidly is becoming a recognized poetry scholar through her publications. She's been a real coup for him."

"How does the rest of the faculty feel about the way he treats her? Aren't they jealous of her arrangement?"

"I really don't know," Bill said as he kicked an acorn in front of them. "I've tried to keep a fairly low profile since I became a student, but I do know that there are a lot of them scrounging for tenure this year."

"Is that low profile why you don't have your picture in the freshman yearbook?" Denney asked.

"The freshman yearbook?"

"I mean the freshman annual. When Kellie and I were looking up names and faces to identify for my teaching gig in Harris' class, we went through the annual. It has your name, but only a 'No picture available' notation."

"You just figured it out, 'No picture available.' I don't remember being asked to submit a picture for anything."

"They used the picture we sent in with our application."

"Honest, I don't remember ever sending a picture. If I did send one with my application, maybe they lost it. Look, there is a lot you don't know about me, but there is a lot I don't know about you, either. I'll share anything you want to know about Bill Smythe, if you'll let me get to know the mystery behind your smile."

Denney blushed, but smiled. Bill pressed on. "There is a Sinclair rally at Crisler Arena next Friday night. Would you like to go with me?"

"A Sinclair rally?"

"Yeah, John Sinclair was one of the SDS guys here back in the sixties. They knew he was into campus protest stuff, but they never could prove anything violent. They got him and put him away because he was in possession of two jays, you know marijuana cigarettes."

"I know," Denney said.

"They threw the book at him. He's still serving time."

"But I thought Ann Arbor has a five dollar misdemeanor law?" Even though Denney didn't really care what the law on the subject was, she was sure she had read that Ann Arbor had passed its own ordinance that was completely different than the rest of the state.

"It does, now. After his arrest, some of his friends who

were on the city council were able to get the five dollar law passed so that getting busted with a small amount of marijuana is no worse on your record and no more expensive than a parking ticket, but the law didn't retroactively cover Sinclair. His friends have been arranging different kinds of protests on his behalf. Friday's concert is going to have some big music names performing. Instead of being paid, all the money is being donated to the Sinclair legal defense fund. They've advertised that Commander Cody will be performing. So, will you go with me?"

"Sure." Denney was pleased. Even though she hadn't been able to read the signs, apparently Kellie was right about Bill being interested in her.

"Great. Parking near Crisler Arena is even worse than here, so we'd be better off walking. Let's grab an early dinner before the concert. I know a good hole in the wall, Lou's, just a few blocks from the arena. Lou makes a great burger."

"Sounds good to me. It will break up the feeling that our walk is some form of exercise."

Bill laughed. "We wouldn't want to give that impression, would we? Here we are," he said as they approached a group of glass doors on the Mason Hall side of the building. Each one they tried was locked. Denney began to walk back towards the parked car, but Bill motioned her to follow him around the building, closer to where Angell Hall merged into Mason Hall. He began counting bushes. Stepping behind a tall bush, he reached out and using a pushing/pulling motion, he undid the latch of a small door that had been obscured by the bush. "Voila," he said softly. "Always a way in."

# FOURTEEN

"WE'RE BREAKING AND entering," Denney said, not moving.

"Not breaking, just entering. Believe it or not, this door has been open like this since the beginning of time." As she looked at him skeptically, he continued, "Or at least since my Dad was here. This used to be some kind of custodial room for the maze of steam tunnels that run under the campus. It hasn't been used in years except as an entrance to the building, when needed. Come on, let's go see if Helen is here. Just remember, if we run into Fred, the guard, act like you're supposed to be here. Follow my lead."

"Sure." Right to jail, she thought, as she trailed Bill into a small room that looked like nobody had disturbed the dust in quite awhile. Closing the door, he strolled across the empty room with a confidence and sense of knowledge that made Denney realize he had done this often. Together, they walked up a Mason Hall stairway and then turned into the main Angell Hall lobby. As they waited for the elevator, they heard footsteps coming from the opposite direction. Bill gave Denney a meaningful glance as Fred came into sight.

"What are you…." Fred began. "Oh, it's you, Mr. Smythe. You back again?"

"Yes, Fred. We were just going upstairs to see if we could catch Professor Willoughby or Ms....."

"Manchester," Denney supplied.

"Haven't seen them lately, but there's been a lot of folks in and out tonight. Help yourself," he said pointing to the elevator as its doors opened.

"Have a good weekend, Fred," Bill called as they got into the elevator. As the doors closed, Denney thought she heard Fred reply, "You too, Mr. Smythe," but she wasn't sure. Once the rubber stoppers of the doors eased shut, Denney and Bill looked at each other and burst out laughing. "Told you there is always a way to get in." He pushed the elevator button.

With a slight shudder, the elevator began its ascent. Denney noted that, "To listen to Fred, you'd think this was Grand Central Station tonight."

"Could be," Bill replied, putting his hand out to insure that the elevator doors stayed open on the English department's floor. As she stepped out of the elevator, Denney stopped for a moment to get her bearings. "Willoughby's office is about midway down this hall," Bill said.

"I know. He's two doors away from Dr. Harris. I saw his name on his door the other day when I was looking for her office."

"Looks like Helen might still be here. There's a light on," Bill said. Catching up with Bill, Denney pushed the partially closed door open. "Hey, Helen, we've come to res...."

"Helen isn't here," Professor Willoughby said. Sitting at his desk, strewn with proof pages, he looked at them from over his reading glasses. "From the look of it, she hasn't been here all evening."

"But she was earlier," Bill insisted. "I saw her when I was up here before the party."

"She was, but it doesn't look like she stayed around once I left for your party. Except for restacking part of these proofs in some order only she understands, everything is in shambles. It will take me the rest of the night to put these pages in some semblance of order so that I can edit them to meet my deadline. Now, if you'll excuse me, I have quite a bit to do."

"Can we help?" Denney asked, wondering where Helen had gone.

"No. Thank you anyway," he said, shuffling the papers on his desk. "I really must…."

The final part of his sentence was blocked out by a piercing scream that increased in volume as Bill and Denney rushed back into the hallway. Looking in both directions, they realized the scream, which had now become a singsongy moan, was coming from Dr. Harris' office. Almost tripping over each other, they stopped short, staring at Dr. Harris' back. Peering around Bill's shoulder, Denney could make out something on the floor on the far side of her desk.

Sensing their presence, Dr. Harris turned towardsthem and the noise stopped. "My God," she said in a hoarse whisper as she pushed past them out of the office.

Denney looked back at Dr. Harris, now leaning on the wall across from her office, while Bill walked closer towards the spot behind her desk that had been Dr. Harris' focus. Bending down slowly, he gingerly reached his hand out, pushing aside the edge of the blue scarf covering Helen's neck. He quickly pulled his hand back. Denney started to kneel beside him, but he turned and said, "Denney, don't. It's Helen. Go back to Willoughby's office and call the police. She's dead." Bill gently guided her up and out of the office. "Go call the police. I'll make sure nobody comes in, leaves, or touches anything."

Back in the hallway, Denney stared at him, framed by the doorway, and then at Dr. Harris, who still leaned against the wall, clutching a bookend in her hand. Following Denney's eyes, Dr. Harris looked at her fingers as if seeing them for the first time, then uncurled them dropping the bookend. For a moment, the two of them just looked at the Chaucer bookend now resting against Denney's boot.

Denney turned and rushed back to Willoughby's office. As she did, she saw a few other faculty members, apparently also working late, coming down the hall in search of the source of the scream. She found him sitting behind his desk sorting proofs, oblivious to the noise around him. "Call the police. It's Helen. In Dr. Harris' office."

Willoughby didn't move.

"Call the police now!" Denney repeated.

# FIFTEEN

*Sunday, December 5, 1971*

IT SEEMED, FROM Denney's perspective, that Helen was being lost in a turf battle between campus security and the police, but then an Ann Arbor Police detective, who introduced himself as Sergeant Jim Rutledge, assumed jurisdiction. Quietly, he began giving orders. He sent two uniformed officers and two campus security people to check for other people on the floor, and then in the building. He also directed Fred to place chairs in the hallway near the elevator bank for Willoughby, Bill, Harris, Denney and the other people still on the floor.

"But I need to work," Professor Willoughby protested. "Surely, I can sit in my own office instead of the hallway!" Politely, Sergeant Rutledge refused his request and motioned for another officer to guide Willoughby to the chairs. Undeterred, Willoughby pulled his chair back towards the elevator bank and began complaining to any police-type person who came within earshot.

Bill talked in low tones attempting to comfort Dr. Harris. Denney blocked out their conversation, trying to recall what she had seen. In her mind, she saw part of a body lying behind the desk and a stain in the carpet, but Bill hadn't actually let her get close enough to see Helen's face. It felt unreal, but even if she was making it all up, Dr. Harris' almost ashen color had been very real as had her shock when she stared back into her office, bookend in hand.

Why, Denney thought, looking at Dr. Harris, would she have killed Helen? They were friends. Helen had told her so. But the image of Dr. Harris with the bookend in her hand persisted, contradicting everything.

Hearing a ruckus down the hall, Denney looked up and realized that Willoughby had again left his seat to argue with Sergeant Rutledge, who apparently had been interviewing the faculty members working in the offices on the other end of the floor. From where she sat, Denney recognized Mrs. Henderson and Mr. Godbolt, but she wasn't sure who the other two teachers clustered with them were.

As the tone of the conversation between Sergeant Rutledge and Willoughby elevated, Bill got up and walked towards them. Dr. Harris looked straight at Denney. "I know what you're thinking," she said. Denney bit her tongue not to respond. She tried to keep her face from showing any sign of what she was thinking. "I didn't hurt Helen. She was my friend."

"If you didn't do it, who did kill her?" Denney asked.

"I don't know. She was fine when I saw her in Willoughby's office earlier this evening, except for being snowed under by the stack of proofs that she needed to edit tonight. When I left to go home, she was stacking them by number so she could review them in order."

"What time was that?"

"About seven. I still haven't quite shaken this bug, so I decided to go home and curl up with a good book. Before I left, I poked my head into Willoughby's office. I wanted to tell Helen that I needed a teatime rain check."

"Teatime?"

"Helen and I take a break together about ten. Because

I always drink tea, I dubbed it teatime. I said good-night and left her working."

"And?" Denney prodded.

"And that's it. I said good-night and left." She wiped a tear from her face with the same hand that had held the bookend.

"So, how did she get into your office? Don't you always lock it?"

Dr. Harris paused for a moment. "I didn't tonight. Helen mentioned that her throat felt a little scratchy so I told her I'd go back and leave my door unlocked in case she wanted a cup of tea to soothe it. I asked her to make sure she pulled my door shut when she left."

"Did you come back to make sure the door was closed?"

"No, after I got home, I was reading and fell asleep. When I woke up, I was wide awake and felt better than I have all week. I decided to come back and get some work done. Maybe subconsciously I was worried about my office being unlocked, but I really wanted to catch up on my work. When I walked into my office, I saw Helen lying there and then I saw the blood. That's when I started screaming."

"And the bookend?"

Dr. Harris shook her head. "I remember saying her name and reaching down towards her. I must have picked the bookend up. It all happened so fast." She covered her eyes with her hands and bent forward.

"But if you only were here a few minutes, Bill and I should have seen you going down the hall. After all, we were in Willoughby's office."

"That explains why you didn't see me," she said, looking back up at Denney. "I didn't come from that direction. I'm a little afraid of these elevators." She glanced at the closed doors. "They have a tendency to get stuck. Call it paranoia or whatever, I usually take the steps. Most of us here do."

Before Denney could ask anything else, Sergeant Rutledge and Bill interrupted them. "Have you found out anything yet?" Denney inquired as she looked down the hall to where another officer was talking to Willoughby.

"Not much. We'll know more in a few hours when we get some initial test results back. For now, let me see if I understand what you two were doing here tonight so I can make some notes, and let you get home to bed."

Bill and Denney quickly explained that they had come to see if Helen was finished and would like to join them for a late night snack. With tacit understanding, they omitted describing how they had gotten into the building, but told Officer Rutledge about running into Fred, popping in on Willoughby instead of Helen, and then hearing the screaming. Denney also provided Sergeant Rutledge with general information about Helen's parents, whom she had met on a few occasions when they both lived at Markley.

Closing his little red notebook, Sergeant Rutledge dismissed Bill and Denney with some movie-like jargon about staying available in case he had further questions, and then he turned his attention to Dr. Harris. As he began to talk with her in a voice different than he had used with Bill and Denney, he realized that they were still there. "I told you, you two can leave."

"We're waiting for Dr. Harris," Bill said. "I thought we could either take her home or walk her to her car."

"She could be awhile," Rutledge replied. "We'll make sure she gets home safely."

"Are you questioning her as a suspect?" Bill asked. He moved away from Denney.

Sergeant Rutledge squared off opposite Bill. "I'm just trying to get some general information. You didn't seem to have any objections a few minutes ago."

"But you didn't treat us like suspects."

"For now, everyone, including you, is a suspect. Look, kid, I'm just trying to do my job and figure out what happened here. I would think instead of getting in the way, you'd want to let us find out what happened to your friend. Now, come on, I've got to talk with Dr. Harris now."

"I'm not trying to be disrespectful, sir, but I don't think Dr. Harris should answer any more questions without her lawyer being present."

"A lawyer. I don't need a lawyer," Dr. Harris protested. "I didn't do anything except walk into my office and find Helen lying on my floor. You believe me, don't you?" Dr. Harris raised her head and looked at Bill. "I didn't do anything wrong. I have nothing to hide."

"That's right," Sergeant Rutledge said. "If she just clears up a few things we can move on tonight." Rutledge took a step to put himself between Dr. Harris and Bill.

Bill ignored him. He again pleaded with Dr. Harris. "Suzanne, I really think you shouldn't answer anything without a lawyer present. I'm pretty sure Dad will send someone to represent you from the firm."

She nodded.

Bill cleared his throat. "Sergeant Rutledge, representation will be arranged through Garan, Smythe, Rogers, and Simpson." Although Denney had not heard of the law firm, Sergeant Rutledge's face showed signs that he recognized the name.

"I think the three of us should all leave now," Bill said.

"Not so fast, Mr. Smythe. Unless I miss my guess, you're not the Smythe in the firm of Garan, Smythe,

Rogers, and Simpson nor, for that matter, are you a licensed attorney. Consequently, I would recommend that you not practice law without a license," he said dismissively. "Whether here or at the station, Dr. Harris and I still have a number of things to discuss."

As Bill began to object again, Dr. Harris shook her head. Stopping his protest, Bill stepped closer to Dr. Harris, and placed a hand on her shoulder. He bent down and quietly reminded her: "Suzanne, please don't say anything else. I'll call Dad as soon as we get downstairs, and he'll get somebody to represent you. It'll be okay." Without glancing back at Rutledge, Bill turned and began to walk towards the elevator with Denney following close behind.

# SIXTEEN

*Sunday, December 5, 1971*

ONCE ON THE first floor of the building, Bill went to the telephone bank to call his father while Denney waited in the lobby. From where she was standing, she could see part of Bill's arm and back as he talked. Alone, she paced back and forth in front of the elevators. Every sound in the building was making her jumpy. Helen was dead and Denney felt certain that there had been more to the warnings Helen had given her over the past few weeks. She decided she would feel more comfortable waiting closer to Bill.

As she began to walk towards the phone bank, she heard a distinct click to her right. Startled by the sound, she turned her head and looked across the lobby. Both the elevator and the stairwell doors were closed. Crossing by the last elevator, she stopped again as the door opened revealing Willoughby on his knees picking up books and papers scattered across the elevator floor.

"Professor Willoughby! Are you all right?" Before he could answer, the elevator door began to close. Denney instinctively stuck her hand between the closing doors, causing them to reopen. She stifled a laugh at the image of Professor Willoughby riding the elevator indefinitely as he sorted through his jumbled papers. No wonder Helen had been putting in so many hours; she had had to organize him and do his work.

Banishing random memories of Helen from her mind, she reached to help Willoughby pick up his papers. He now was sitting with his back against the wall of the elevator. The doors, no longer blocked, closed as she began picking up the papers scattered haphazardly on the elevator floor. With a slight jerk, the elevator began to ascend.

"Be careful with those sheets," Professor Willoughby warned, oblivious to the now upward motion of the elevator as it responded to whoever had summoned it. Denney randomly picked up the fallen pages. "I need to get them back in numeric order," Willoughby said. Denney looked at the paper in her hand noting that it was marked P221 in the right hand corner.

"Do you want them by letter or number?"

"Number. What do you think numeric order is? There might be twenty-six pages with the same letter. It's a dictionary, you know."

"Sorry," she said, as she began sorting the pages by number. "I always thought dictionaries have more letters at the top of each page. More like Mon-Mop, not just a singular alphabet letter."

"That's when a dictionary is finished," he replied. "Until you know exactly what is on the page, you can't sub-alphabetize it. That's what Helen was doing tonight. She was matching our original text against the proof pages we got today, and then was going to assign the final alphabetical letters for each completed dictionary proof page. If she had finished, we would have been well ahead of schedule, but I don't know what she did. Everything is in shambles."

Denney gently removed the few pages he still clutched in his hand and began interspersing them with those she had picked up. Willoughby slumped against the elevator wall. "It's hopeless. I shall never meet Ferguson's deadline now."

"We can get these back in order."

"Even if you do, it won't matter. The police have the actual dictionary proofs."

"Why?"

"I don't know. I told them that they were all out of order and that I needed to continue sorting them out, but that Sergeant Rutledge insisted…" The elevator jolted. The doors opened to reveal Mrs. Henderson. Denney barely saved two pieces of paper from ending up under Mrs. Henderson's right foot as she stepped into the elevator, ignoring the pages and the two of them sprawled on the floor. She firmly pressed the first floor button. "Brenda, what are you doing here? I took you home," Willoughby said.

"That you did," she said as the door opened into the lobby. She walked out of the elevator, past a perplexed-looking Bill. Jumping to her feet, Denney shoved the papers she was holding at Bill and rushed to follow Mrs. Henderson out of the building. "Where are you going?" Bill called.

"Be back in a minute. Help Professor Willoughby," she yelled back over her shoulder as she pushed the exit bar to leave the building. "Mrs. Henderson! Mrs. Henderson. Please stop."

Mrs. Henderson turned back towards Denney. "What? Debbie, isn't it?"

"Denney. You know Helen was killed tonight…" Denney began.

"Oh yes. Tragic. I found out when I went upstairs. I'm really not in the mood to stand here and chitchat with you."

"It will only take a minute," Denney pleaded as she

moved closer to Mrs. Henderson. "I only wanted to know if you happened to see her tonight. You know, you both were working on the dictionary."

"Of course I saw Helen." Mrs. Henderson took a step back.

"You did?"

"We all did, earlier tonight. Before the party. Willoughby and I saw her working in his office. In fact, that is what I was just thinking about. It was the last time I saw Helen. She was such a lovely girl. A hard worker. I can't believe she's gone. She was such a dear friend." Her voice cracked. "I really don't feel like talking now. It's too cold." She pulled her coat tighter around her exposed neck and began walking down the path towards the Diag.

Denney didn't try to stop her. Instead, she returned to the building, where Bill was waiting at the glass doors for her. Professor Willoughby was nowhere to be seen.

"Denney, I need to take you home. They're going to take Suzanne downtown for questioning and Dad wants me to meet him there. He is going to represent her if she needs it."

Denney stared at him for a second and then the two began walking towards the car in silence. Bill opened the door for her. "Denney, are you okay?" he asked.

"Am I okay? What kind of question is that? One of my best friends has been murdered. All I can think about and all that I'm trying not to think about is Helen. No, I'm not okay. Faculty members are acting as though they are characters in a bad mystery novel, and every time I turn around, you seem to have another surprise connection to one of them. Helen's parents don't even know their daughter is dead, and you're already arranging for her murderer to be represented by your father!"

"That's exactly why I called Dad. People jumping to conclusions about Dr. Harris."

"Conclusions? We saw her with the bookend in her hand!"

"Denney, Suzanne is not a murderer. She and Helen were friends. Helen would have wanted her other friends to take care of her, not to jump to conclusions."

"How can you be so blind? We found her standing in the office."

"I think you're the one being blind. Just because Suzanne Harris found Helen doesn't mean she hurt Helen anymore than we did."

"Just take me home, please."

"Fine, I will." Although Bill watched the road, he kept glancing at Denney who stared out the window. As they pulled into the Sorosis driveway, he softly said, "Denney, please give Dr. Harris a chance. You were Helen's friend. Let's find out who really killed her."

"And if it was Dr. Harris?"

"Then, it will be her, but let's not prejudge the situation. Please?" Bill stopped the car in front of the sorority house behind a white car. Its brake lights gleamed like eyes in the dark. The front passenger door opened, illuminating the outline of a man in the driver's seat and a woman. Denney could only see her back as she slid out, barely getting both feet on the ground before the car lurched forward, slamming the passenger door closed and making her stumble. Without looking back, she regained her balance and ran up the steps. As she opened the door, the overhead porch light briefly lit her shadowed face.

"What do you make of that?" Denney asked when Kellie had disappeared into the house.

"I don't," Bill replied. "That's their private business. Sometimes it's better to leave things private."

"Like your picture in the freshman annual?" Bill started to respond but she cut him off as she opened her car door. "Sorry. You've made your point and while I don't agree with you about Dr. Harris, I'm willing, for Helen's sake, to try to be open-minded. Let me know what happens tonight."

"I'll call you as soon as I know anything. Good night."

"Good night," Denney said as she shut the door. She waved at Bill. She was anxious to get into the house and find Kellie. It was time to get some answers.

# SEVENTEEN

*Sunday, December 5, 1971*

THE HOUSE WAS quiet, but Denney was determined to find Kellie, even if it meant waking Ana. Except for a single lamp illuminating the stairs, the main floor was dark. She stood still—listening. Everything was silent. Standing in the lobby, she glanced into the dining room. It was empty. As she started up the first two steps, she thought she heard a sound coming from her left. Stopping, she listened again. Denney stepped back into the lobby to get a better view of the downstairs rooms.

Even though the rooms were dark, Denney found herself drawn to the library. Walking quietly, she heard a mew-like sound coming from the couch that Denney herself often hid on. Moving quickly, Denney crossed the rest of the living room and stood outside the library arch. Muffled crying definitely was coming from the library. Hearing the sobs, Denney debated whether to intrude or go to her room. She decided she really had no choice.

"Can I help?" she asked as she saw the mound of a body pressed into the cushions.

"No, go away," came the reply from deep in the pillows of the couch. "There's nothing you can do," Kellie said, slightly raising her head. Seeing her friend's tear-stained face, Denney's anger from the past few days slipped away. She sat on the sofa next to Kellie and put her arms around her.

"Nothing can be that bad, Kellie. Let me help you."

"You can't."

"Try me. Maybe together we can puzzle out whatever it is."

"Not this time."

"Come on Kellie, I'm your friend." Denney realized that she actually meant it. "Friendship is built on trust, respect, and sharing. If you can't talk to me, then let me get Ana. You obviously need to talk to someone."

"I can't. You guys will hate me." Kellie began to cry heavily, her body shaking.

"Kell, does this have something to do with Dr. Ferguson?" Kellie nodded. "Did he hurt you?"

"He…" Kellie took a deep breath to control her sobbing.

"If he hurt you, we'll kill him!" Denney said. Events of the night came flooding back, but she made herself shake off thoughts of Helen to concentrate on what Kellie was saying.

Kellie laughed. "You'll have to take a place in line." She pulled away from Denney and walked across the room, her arms wrapped around herself. Kellie stared at the books perfectly arranged on the white painted bookshelves. She pulled out one from just off center. The other books tilted to fill the opening she had created. "Do you know how I became a boarder at Sorosis?"

"No."

"I became a boarder because Ferguson told me Sorosis had good food, a very reasonable rate, and most importantly, he could arrange a place for me even though school had begun."

"Dr. Ferguson arranged for you to live here? I didn't realize you were friends with him before transferring to the University."

"Not exactly friends. Denney, this is the hard part. Promise me, no matter what I tell you now, you'll hear me out before you pass judgment on me. Promise?"

"I promise." Denney waited quietly for Kellie to continue.

"Ferguson is, or was," Kellie hesitated, "more than my friend."

"Ferguson?"

"Denney, please," Kellie implored.

"I'm listening," Denney said, trying to stay focused while her mind tried to process the implication of what Kellie had just said. "I won't say another word until you're done."

# EIGHTEEN

*Sunday, December 5, 1971*

"YOU REMEMBER HOW I've told you about my great Irish household?"

Denney nodded, but said nothing.

"Well, there are a few details that I left out of the version that you know. I guess you might say it is the reality of the O'Reilly household that I conveniently forgot to share with Ana and you." Kellie turned to face Denney, displaying the cover of the book she still held in her hand.

"We could be a novel. In fact, my mother is literature. She grew up loving books and words. As a child, she escaped the rigors of the Catholic schools she went to by weaving the stories she read into her daydreams. My dad was just the opposite. Blond, blue-eyed, with a swagger that made everybody notice him, he was a standout athlete, especially in basketball. Basketball inter-school rivalry with the other Catholic schools gave all the nuns something to pray about for two months every year. The school's basketball program also offered guys like my dad the chance to get college scholarships rather than end up working nightshift at the car assembly plants like their fathers."

Denney couldn't imagine what this had to do with Dr. Ferguson, but she kept quiet, letting Kellie tell it her own way.

"When Dad was a senior, his team made it into the

finals against their archrival, St. Xavier's. University of
Detroit was recruiting him with a good probability of
playing time as a freshman, but there still was a chance
that Michigan State or the University of Michigan might
consider him. You can imagine how much praying was
going on—on both sides of the court when it was a one
point game with three seconds to spare. Dad's team was
down a point but because of a foul, they were throwing
the ball in from the sidelines. Dad was supposed to run
for the far corner and not be a part of the play, but something made him pull up just short of the painted circle.
Glancing back, he saw the guard desperately toss the ball
in. Dad reached up as the ball arched near him. He managed to catch it, pivot, dribble, and get the winning shot
off, but he came down off balance. He hit the court with
such a sickening crunch that Dad immediately knew his
leg was broken. The game and Dad's hopes of playing
college ball ended at the same time."

"But he still could have gone to college," Denney said.

"He didn't have the money or the grades. Besides, I
think he figured without basketball he would be a big
nobody. He ended up getting a GED, going to work at
the plant and hanging around the neighborhood pub a little too regularly. There always seemed to be somebody
there who remembered that last game and was willing
to buy him a beer. The only day his pattern changed was
on Sunday."

"Why was Sunday different? Your dad doesn't sound
religious."

"He wasn't, but my grandmother was. She insisted
that Dad get up and go to morning mass with her. You
didn't mess with my grandmother," Kellie laughed as
she wiped away the tears on her cheek. "While he lived
in her house, Dad never missed mass or the monthly

Sunday night social. Dad claims his reward for going to all those church socials was meeting the prettiest green-eyed redhead in the state of Michigan." Kellie smiled.

"Dad had to work fast. She was spending her summer vacation answering phones for her father's plumbing company before going back to a small liberal arts college in Albion. Mom always has said that but for some bad breaks, Dad could have been a millionaire because he never met a stranger he couldn't sell something to. Obviously, he sold her a bill of goods, because she was pregnant before the end of the summer. They got married over Labor Day. Apparently, my grandfather had a better sales touch."

"Apparently," Denney agreed.

Kellie sat back down on the sofa next to Denney. "Tommy was born about eight months after their wedding. I was born a year later. Bridgette, Rory, Cary, and Kevin were spaced out over the following five years. Can you imagine what it was like in our house with six kids under the age of seven? There was always some loud disaster in the making. Mom put up with whatever we did plus read us stories, wiped away our tears, and cleaned up our messes, but not Dad. He started getting home later and later. We learned early to listen if he was singing or not."

"Singing? Why would that matter?"

"If he was singing, he'd wake us up and be sloppy and sweet to Tommy and me." Kellie averted her eyes from Denney's. She paused, staring at her knees. "I guess that's how I learned to get by without a lot of sleep."

She tried to laugh, but it sounded like a stifled sob. Denney waited for her to continue.

"Those nights were better than the ones when he wasn't singing. Then, he would go straight to their bedroom and usually be so drunk he'd pass out. If he didn't, he would scream at mom until the screaming became something else. The older we got, his jobs changed more often and there hardly was any singing."

"Oh, Kellie, how awful. Couldn't your mom or any of you kids make him stop?"

"It wasn't that easy. Tommy and I helped Mom with the little ones, and we both were good students, but at night we would just lay there praying he would leave her alone. At least we did until one night when I was fifteen. I don't know what was different about that night, but when his voice escalated, I got up and went into their room. My mother was half-crouched next to the bed, and well, it wasn't pretty. I yelled at him to stop, and he turned on me. I had never given him any reason to think it, but he began calling me a whore and slut, but unlike my mother, I didn't just stay quiet and take it."

As she spoke, Kellie got a scary look in her eyes. "I started yelling back telling him what a terribly mean abusive person he was. I got right in his face, and I guess I pushed him a little too hard. He slapped me. My mother was screaming while Dad just stood there looking at his hand. At that moment, Tommy burst into the room and tackled him to the floor. They were rolling on the floor, while I just sat on the bed with my hand on my cheek trying to figure out why it felt like separate stings where each of his fingers had made contact." Kellie shuddered. Denney put her arm around her again.

"We never discussed that night. My mother acted as if it never happened, but there was one difference. Dad stopped waking any of us, including Mom." Kellie pulled away from Denney and sat straight up, her fists clenched. "I vowed that night that none of us kids, especially me, would ever put up with that kind of abuse. It might mean a lot of work, but for us there would be no factory or living through books." She sighed. "You know what the irony is?"

"No, what?" Denney whispered.

"The irony is we're following in their footsteps. My brother, Tommy, graduated with academic honors, won a partial scholarship to Michigan, and got a full ride to the summer poetry workshop."

"But, he's not at school here, is he?"

"No, he's living at home and working at the car plant while he finds his poetic voice. After Michigan's summer workshop, he decided he already understood the beauty of words and ideas so living in the real world would help him be a better poet instead of attending classes taught by people who never really quite made it. What's scary is that for him, I think he's right. Here's a guy who looks like a prizefighter, and has the sensitivity to be an Irish poet."

"And you?" Denney slipped back into the couch cushions.

"I'm here as an English major thanks to the help of Dr. Ferguson. He came to visit us after he couldn't believe that Tommy wasn't going to enroll in his English program."

"Dr. Ferguson came to your house?"

"Yep. Bow tie and all. He argued that Tommy had the type of talent that if nurtured would easily win Michigan Hopwood Writing Awards and eventually lead to greater literary circle recognition. He made a good pitch to my parents, but couldn't sell Tommy. The two of them finally agreed that Tommy might reconsider Michigan in the future, but for now, they would keep in touch and Dr. Ferguson would help him if he could. There is a lot I don't like about Dr. Ferguson, but he has been great to

Tommy. He initiated some contacts for him with a few literary magazine editors that have resulted in Tommy having two of his poems published. He only got paid in copies, but Tommy feels both journals are prestigious enough to be a good career start. For that, my parents and Tommy are grateful to Ferguson."

"And you? How did you get so involved with him?

"Innocently. I thought he was helping me like he had helped Tommy. My grades were good enough to get into Michigan and Wayne State, but only Wayne State offered me scholarship money. I started going there, but hated it. Without telling me, Tommy called Dr. Ferguson to find out whether there might be any Michigan scholarship money or work study available for me. Knowing Dr. Ferguson like I now do, I guess he figured he could make Tommy feel indebted to him if he helped me. Anyway, he came to ourhouse again, supposedly to critique a poem Tommy was submitting for publication to another magazine. Before he left, he suggested to my parents and me that I come to Ann Arbor for lunch the next day as there might be some funds available so I could transfer. I jumped at the chance. In hindsight, I knew what was going on because I took my time dressing and putting my makeup on. We met in his office and then he took me to Webers for lunch."

"My parents always take me there when they're in town. It's really good," Denney said.

"My folks never have taken me there but I'd heard so much about it that I was impressed from the moment I saw the burgundy tablecloths. After we sat down, Ferguson got right to the point. He said I would make an excellent student, but there no longer were too many scholarship or work study opportunities available. I guess I must have looked a little disappointed as I played with my salad because he reached over and placed his hand over mine. I was torn between looking down at my hand or making eye contact, but I decided to go with the eye contact. So, I ignored where his hand had wandered.

"He didn't move his hand as he explained that although nothing was available through formal channels, he had enough discretionary departmental funds to cover my tuition by hiring me as a student research assistant to his staff. For that much money, I was concerned what would be expected of me." Kellie paused.

Denney didn't move for fear of interrupting Kellie.

"He assured me that my duties would be clerical—typing, filing, or proofreading, until I was further along in my studies. I concentrated on my London Broil when he noted that the job might even help me find a direction for my studies like it had for Mrs. Henderson."

"So, why didn't you say yes? Being a research assistant has to be easier than the hours you work at The Jugg."

"I did say yes." Kellie got up and put the book back in bookcase. With her back to Denney, she whispered, "To everything he asked."

# NINETEEN

*Sunday, December 5, 1971*

DENNEY SAT STUNNED. Kellie waited for her to say something, but Denney wasn't sure what to say. She stood up and walked over to Kellie. "Everything?" she finally asked.

"Everything. I think Cher had us in mind when she sang that song about what would have happened if her daddy knew what she was doing. When my dad overheard me on the phone with Dr. Ferguson, he didn't say a word. Just got into his car and drove to Ann Arbor. He got to Ferguson's office and had just confronted him when Willoughby and Henderson arrived for some dictionary meeting. Dr. Ferguson used the two of them as a means of getting Dad out of his office before anything more happened."

"As mad as your dad was, he just left?"

"Oh, he was boiling, but before he threw a punch, he at least had the intelligence to control himself and leave before things got worse."

"So, that was the end of it?"

"Not by a long shot," Kellie said. "He got home and came straight to my room. I was sitting in front of my vanity putting on makeup." Her gaze drifted from Denney. "I was holding a plum lip pencil preparing to outline my upper lip when he came into my room. I just sat there holding that pencil and waited. I didn't move. He raised his arm as if he was going to hit me, but then he just swept everything off my vanity. My makeup, perfume bottles, a glass of water. Everything crashed against the floor and wall speckling them with damp blotches and a lingering sick sweet smell from the mixing of the perfumes." She looked back at Denney.

"I didn't try to protect myself when he bent his arm again. Subconsciously, I think I felt I deserved to be hit. I was waiting for the blow, but it never came. With the same fluid motion he had used on my vanity, he pulled his hand back towards his face, and Denney, he was crying. He stood there looking at me through tears. It was worse than if he had hit me. All his strength and bluster were gone. I stood up and instinctively reached to hug him, but he stepped back."

"What happened then?" Denney coaxed Kellie to continue.

"Nothing. Tommy heard the noise and came barreling into my room. I guess he thought he was going to have to pull Dad off of me, but there was nothing for him to do. Dad looked from me to Tommy and then back at me. Although his eyes were on my face, he talked to Tommy in a hoarse voice, I had never heard. 'Get her out of here. Take her to him. *Now.*'

"'Dad!' I screamed after him, trying to follow him from the room, but he pulled the door shut behind him. We haven't talked since." Kellie sobbed and buried her face in Denney's shoulder.

When Kellie's tears eased, Denney leaned back so she could see her face. "Oh, Kellie, I can't imagine what it has been like for you. I don't know how you've been able to make it."

"I don't think about it. Tommy convinced me I had to take a few things and go back to Ann Arbor before Dad got back. He assured me that he would clean up and bring the rest of my clothes later. We went straight to Dr. Ferguson's office. He didn't want me either," she laughed.

"But I've seen you with Dr. Ferguson."

"Only superficially. He told us there was nothing more he would do for me. Tommy heard him out and then calmly told him he had promised an education to me, and he expected him to honor it. Ferguson said there was no way that I could work for him now, but Tommy said that didn't matter as long as he helped me find a place to stay and made sure my tuition was taken care of."

"Tommy blackmailed Dr. Ferguson? With what?" Denney stood with her hands on her hips incredulous at what she was hearing.

"It wasn't exactly blackmail. You might say he exerted pressure in a quid pro quo exchange for services already rendered. As the two of them bartered, I felt like a cheap whore. Ferguson blinked first. He picked up the phone, and I guess he either called an alum or the Sorosis housemother, because he hung up, grabbed a pad, and wrote down the Sorosis address. He handed it to me saying, 'They're expecting you. Sorosis is taking boarders and your room and board will be covered for the first semester. After that, you're on your own. Same with tuition after this year,' he said looking at Tommy."

"So you are using The Jugg for living expenses, but Ferguson is covering your tuition through next term?" Denney thought back to the conversation Ana had overheard. It seemed that it might have something to do with this.

"More or less. He managed to find grants and other things to cover my tuition last semester, but he didn't pay anything for this term. The registrar's office notified me last week my bill was overdue. I immediately called Ferguson, but he didn't return my phone calls and when I went up to his office, he either wasn't there or was too busy to see me. I scraped together whatever I could from my Jugg money and selling back my old textbooks to make a payment on my account so they would let me stay in school. I also kept trying to get in touch with Ferguson."

"Kellie, Ana and I would have helped you," Denney said.

"Friendship is one thing. Funding my education is another." Kellie put her hand on her friend's shoulder. "Actually, you did help me out."

"I did?" Perplexed, Denney squinted her eyes.

"Yeah. Ferguson finally took one of my calls and acted as if he had never avoided me. He invited me to meet him for breakfast to discuss my tuition. Before I could let him have it with both barrels, Ana walked into our room. I couldn't talk about this in front of her so I ended the call without resolving anything except agreeing to meet him at the University Club for breakfast. I guess he figured I wouldn't make a scene there. That's why I borrowed your gray suit. I had to have something appropriate to wear. You weren't around, but I didn't think you'd care. When I brought it back, I realized you were mad that I had helped myself to your suit, but I couldn't tell you why. I'm sorry."

"It's okay, Kellie. I wish you would have talked to Ana and me. We could have helped."

"I couldn't."

"What happened at breakfast?"

"He laughed at me. Told me I was an idealistic child who needed to learn about the real world," Kellie replied. "Then, as we sat at a table with faculty members on both sides of us and other people that I didn't know, he reached into his inner jacket pocket and pulled out a small box. He said it was nothing much, that he had given every woman in the department the same gift for the holidays last year and he had a few extras. I opened the box to find a bottle of perfume. He encouraged me to put some on. As I did so, he reached into his pocket again, and pulled out five $100 bills. He passed them across the table and said they were the final settlement for services rendered. I was so shocked that I spilled some of the perfume on your jacket."

"Did you take the money?"

"What could I do? It was either take the money and pay my tuition or drop out. I'd already pulled together whatever money I could to keep afloat; so, I took the money and walked out of the University Club with him sitting there laughing at me." Kellie lowered her head and began to cry again.

Denney stroked Kellie's hair and whispered, "It's all right. Kellie, you did what you felt you had to do. But, what now?"

"I don't know," Kellie said as she raised her head and peered at Denney through red-rimmed eyes. "I don't know," she repeated. "I can't go home again. Hopefully, I can find a second job and work straight through the summer to bank enough to start next year."

"Don't worry," Denney said. "We'll figure it out. If Ana, you, and I put our brains together, we can't miss. You won't be going home again," Denney assured her. For a fleeting second, she thought how easy it would have been for Helen to devise a creative way out of this, but she brought her focus back to Kellie. "But I need to understand something. Why did you leave tonight's party with Dr. Ferguson?"

"To avoid a scene. He called me earlier in the day and

told me he realized he had been harsh. He felt we should talk some more. I went to his office before the party, because he wanted me to do some clerical work for him. I was going to use his secretary's desk, but I couldn't type the confidential document he wanted because the whole area filled up with people worried about their impending tenure recommendation deadlines."

"How many people is he messing with?" Denney interrupted.

"Four or five that I know of," Kellie said. "Dr. Harris already was in Dr. Ferguson's office when I got there, but he told me to wait. Willoughby, Henderson, and Godbolt came by his door while I was waiting in the hall. When he saw all of them waiting, he told me we would have to take care of everything later, perhaps during office hours on Monday."

"So, why didn't you just talk at the party?"

"When he came in, I was surprised to see him." Denney remembered how Kellie had actually frozen when Mrs. Henderson and Dr. Ferguson came in. "After you took their coats, I pointed them to the bar. Mrs. Henderson went, but he stayed to talk to me. At first, he was conciliatory. He said that after I did the job he had in mind, there might be other work study or subsistence options. He was the one who suggested leaving the party so that I could do his typing and then we could discuss the other options without all the big ears in the room. I hesitated, but thought it was better for everybody if I gave in and went with him rather than take a chance of him ruining Bill's party."

"He never would have done that," Denney said.

"You don't know him. Anyway, we left the party and went back to his office."

Excited to know that Kellie had been on the English

Department floor before Helen was killed, she interrupted Kellie's story. "Did you see Helen?"

"I'm sorry, Denney. I saw her earlier in the evening, but not the second time I was there. Dr. Ferguson and I went directly to his office. I don't remember seeing anyone except the guard when we first came in."

"Did the guard see you?"

"I doubt it. His back was to us. Why?" Ignoring the question, Denney asked Kellie to tell her what had happened next. "Nothing for awhile. We were talking pleasantly when Ferguson's phone buzzed. He answered it and listened to whoever was on the line and then said he needed to take care of something, but I should wait. He was gone about twenty minutes, and when he came back it was almost as bad as it had been at the University Club. He ridiculed me for believing in happy endings."

"Happy endings?"

"Right, happy endings. I told him this was anything but. I lost my temper and said some harsh things. Déjà vu, I thought he was going to hit me so I shut my mouth." Kellie's face had gone white again. Denney put her arm around her shoulder to support her as she guided her back to the couch.

Kellie seemed to melt into the sofa. She picked up one of the decorative pillows and threw it on the floor. "He didn't hit me. He never ever actually moved out from behind his desk, but I realized at that moment I would never be able to count on him to help me," she said bitterly. "So, I left."

"But, I saw Dr. Ferguson bring you back to the Sorosis house," Denney interrupted.

"He did. I had to let him bring me home. When I went to leave his office, police and other people were all milling around the floor. I didn't want to get involved so I stepped back into one of the doorways. I could see Bill, you, and Dr. Harris huddled together and Willoughby arguing with some sergeant at your end of the corridor. When they started to wheel the empty gurney from the elevator to Dr. Harris' office, I turned away figuring I would go down the stairs near Ferguson's office, but Dr. Ferguson was right there at my elbow. The big police sergeant was coming towards us. Ferguson whispered in my ear: 'Be quiet. Let me do the talking.'"

"Did you?"

"I felt I had no choice. When the policeman reached us, and identified himself as Sergeant Rutledge and told us about Helen, Dr. Ferguson went into an Academy Award performance. He rambled on about poor Helen, and how could this possibly have happened in our wonderful department. His acting about us all being family was overboard, but Rutledge seemed to buy it. Before Rutledge could ask us any questions, Ferguson put on his department chair persona and went into how Helen's parents would need to be contacted. He offered to make the call on behalf of the University, and mentioned he still needed to take me home. Sergeant Rutledge refused Ferguson's offer to call Helen's parents, but he told Dr. Ferguson we could leave. I guess he felt compelled to take me home to make it look good."

"Real good. I saw the drop-off," Denney dryly observed.

"That's right. A real drop-off. Denney, I'm so embarrassed," Kellie confessed. She crossed her arms as if trying to hold herself close. Denney gave her a one-armed squeeze as the two stood up.

"Don't be embarrassed," Denney said. "If you'll let us, your friends will help you get through this." Kellie nodded.

"Now, my first suggestion, no, let's make that my first order is that we both need to get some sleep. We'll get with Ana later. Things will be okay. Believe me?"

"Almost," Kellie said.

"Believe," Denney intoned in her best God imitation.

# TWENTY

*Sunday—After Lunchtime—December 5, 1971*

DENNEY ROLLED OVER on her bed just in time to see her bedroom doorknob turn. "Who is it?" she yelled. The doorknob stopped moving.

"It's us," Ana's voice came through the door. "Kellie and I were worried when you didn't come to lunch." With her propensity to pudge, Denney couldn't understand why her friends would be concerned with her missing a meal.

She propped herself up on her elbow, knocking the article about Helen from the bed to the floor. Dear Ana. That was it! When Ana had left the room what seemed like days instead of hours ago, she had known how upset Denney was over Helen's death. A missed meal was Ana and Kellie's way of checking up on her, as they had no way of knowing that exhausted from a night of crying, Denney simply had slept through lunch.

"Come in. It isn't locked," she yelled as she bent over the edge of the bed to pick up the newspaper.

Ana, followed by Kellie, slipped inside. Their eyes rested on the newspaper in her hand. "It just doesn't make sense," Denney said. She tossed the paper to the end of the bed.

"No, it doesn't," Kellie agreed. "I don't see how the police let Dr. Harris go. Helen was on the floor in her office and Dr. Harris was right there screaming so loudly everyone in the building heard her. I absolutely don't understand why the police didn't immediately arrest her." Denney did not volunteer that she shared Kellie's opinion, especially since Dr. Harris had been holding the bookend.

"I just can't see it," Ana said. "In my book, friends don't kill friends for no apparent reason."

"You sound like Bill. He thinks that in a close situation like this, the tie goes to the runner. Bill keeps insisting that I shouldn't immediately find Dr. Harris guilty as the true facts could go either way. The problem is that I know what I saw."

"What you saw could be circumstantial," Ana suggested. She picked up the article from the bed, careful not to disturb the other things Denney had dropped on the floor.

"Maybe. Bill is convinced that Dr. Harris isn't the kind of person who could ever have murdered Helen. I'm not as sure as he is."

"Me neither," Kellie said.

Ana pointed to the beginning of the article. "From what you've said, why wasn't Helen at the poetry party with you?"

Denney pushed her blankets off and began pacing the room as she explained to Ana that Helen skipped the party to finish some proofreading for Professor Willoughby.

"She was stuck working because he was going back to his office to wrap things up after the party," Kellie explained.

"That's right. When Bill and I first went into Willoughby's office looking for Helen, we found him at his desk trying to sort the proof pages. He thought that except for putting them into some kind of random piles, she hadn't done any work once he left for the party." Rubbing her forehead, which really did hurt, Denney continued.

"That's the first thing I don't understand. I know Helen. She would never have left without finishing what she was getting paid to do. And because she had so much work, I can't understand what she was doing in Harris' office instead of Willoughby's."

"Visiting? Having hot chocolate like we do?" Ana lay the paper down on Denney's makeshift bookcase kitchen and picked up the hot pot the three of them often used to heat water when they shared hot chocolate. She turned it over as if expecting to find something written on it.

"Possibly. Harris claims they had a regular teatime ritual, but they skipped it last night because Dr. Harris didn't stay. If Helen had finished early, she would have come to our party; and knowing Helen, if she had a problem with the proofs, she would have come to the party to find Willoughby."

"That makes sense," Kellie said. "She wouldn't have sat in the office wasting time when she knew Willoughby was at Bill's party and was the type who would probably be one of the last to leave."

Denney and Kellie exchanged a look that Ana missed. As she thought of the last minutes of the party, Denney began rummaging in the top drawer of her dresser. Listening to herself recount the sequence of events, she felt like there was something she had left out, something she had seen that was not right, but she couldn't put her finger on it.

"Maybe she wasn't sure how long he was going to stay at the party," Ana suggested. "I would have thought Willoughby, or any faculty member, would have made a token appearance at best. You know, in and out."

"Ferguson did that," Kellie said, "but Willoughby and Henderson were there to the end."

"What about Dr. Harris?" Ana asked.

"She had that flu bug this week and told Bill she still didn't feel like coming. She brought a dip, but was well gone before any of us got there. Apparently, she had other things to do," Denney said, as she began going through the second drawer in her dresser.

Ana picked up the newspaper again holding it so they all could see the picture of Helen. "Maybe Dr. Harris did have other things to do last night, but thinking of her murdering Helen still doesn't feel right to me."

"Not you, too," Denney moaned. She shook the pill bottle she had just found in her dresser. "Why won't anyone even consider that she could be guilty? I swear all of you are giving me a gigantic headache, and I'm out of aspirin."

"You really have a headache?" Kellie asked.

"Probably lack of sleep or something," Denney dryly observed. She dropped the bottle back into her drawer.

"Either of you have any aspirin upstairs?"

"Ask and you shall receive." Ana grinned. "I'll get you some. Maybe you can go back to bed for an afternoon nap."

After Kellie and Ana left, Denney picked up a shirt from the floor, but rather than sorting the piled mounds on the floor, she decided to call Marta, the chief resident advisor for Mary Markley Dormitory. She technically was Helen's dormitory boss.

Marta already had been Markley's chief advisor for a few years when Denney and Helen were freshmen. She oversaw all dorm operations, including things pertaining to Blagdon and Frost, the sub-dormitory houses to which Denney and Helen had been assigned. Denney was living in the sorority house when Marta hired Helen as a Blagdon hall advisor. At the time, there were many people who felt that Helen's Black Action Movement related activities should preclude her from being a potential role model for incoming freshmen, but Marta had argued that having a different viewpoint was exactly why Helen should be an advisor.

Denney knew that Marta, a country girl from Chelsea, Michigan, was always up at sunrise so there would be no chance of accidentally waking her mid-Sunday. Sure enough, a subdued sounding Marta answered the phone on the first ring. By the time Ana returned with the aspirin, Denney and Marta were deep in conversation. With a nod of appreciation, Denney took the aspirin bottle from her, and motioned for Ana to sit down. Shaking her head, Ana mouthed "Talk to you later."

According to Marta, most of the people in the dormitory knew little more than had been reported in the newspaper. A policewoman had come to the dormitory about 5:00 a.m. seeking access to Helen's room. Marta tried to stay with her, but after having been told her presence was not necessary, she retreated to the small student lounge across the hall from Helen's room. Since the policewoman was in and out in less than thirty minutes, Marta doubted she had found anything relevant.

The only other thing Denney learned during the phone call was that Helen's parents hoped to have the funeral as soon as possible. In fact, if they prevailed in having Helen's body autopsied and released quickly, the service could be held in Detroit as soon as Tuesday. Marta indicated that whenever the service was, a group of friends from the dorm planned to carpool together. She offered to make room for Denney if she wanted to be included. "Please. Just call me back when you know the final arrangements."

Hanging up, Denney went down the hall to the floor's common restroom. Her reflection in the mirror decidedly

looked hungover, but she hadn't had a drink. The dark
circles under her eyes were probably a combination of
her headache and sleep deprivation. Another nap might
make a big difference in how she felt. Sleeping also would
be an escape from thinking about Helen.

Denney ran a mental check of her classes. The only
homework left was the paper for Dr. Harris. Surely Dr.
Harris wouldn't hold class tomorrow, and even if she did,
she would have to give Denney a break. Denney decided
to skip working on the paper and go back to sleep.

She swallowed two aspirin, took the receiver off its
hook, switched off the light, lay down, and instantly fell
into a dreamless sleep. Waking, Denney sat up slowly.
Everything ached and her head felt stuffy. Her clock let
her know she had only been asleep for a couple of hours.

Spotting Ana's aspirin bottle on her desk, Denney
picked it up and shook two more aspirin into her hand.
Swallowing them dry, Denney sat down on the edge of
her bed and analyzed her physical condition. Aching
joints, headache that felt like her hair hurt, stuffy nose,
and a scratchy throat. The only thing lacking was teeth-
chattering chills, but she was freezing. Denney snug-
gled back under her blankets, pulling the comforter close
around her neck, but her efforts to get warm were interrupted by a loud sneeze. Crap, she thought. Dr. Harris
killed Helen, and now, thanks to her own bravado, Dr.
Harris was going to kill her, too.

# TWENTY-ONE

*Monday, December 6, 1971*

BY THE MIDDLE of the night, Denney decided that if she was going to attend Helen's funeral, she could not let herself be as sick as she was pretty sure she was about to be. Not only did her throat feel like the Wolverine football team was running through it in their cleats; she also felt nauseous. Against her better judgment, and so she could get a written excuse for Dr. Harris, Denney was waiting at Student Health Services when it opened. Hopefully, the doctor on duty could give her a shot or some pill that would knock this bug out of her system.

As the Health Services doctor peered into her ears, eyes, nose, and mouth, Denney stared at the little wiry hairs protruding from his ears. She thought that if she had to look at them much longer, she could gag without the need for the tongue depressor he was pushing into her mouth. Finally, after making her garble "aah" twice, he observed that her throat was rather red.

That's an understatement, Denney thought. She stifled the desire to tell him that she didn't need to come to Health Services to know that her throat felt like the site of a cattle drive. Instead of being rude, she agreed. "It definitely hurts.I hope you can give me something to get rid of this bug."

"Not really, it looks like you've got a bad case of the virus that's going around. I can give you something to ease the nausea that comes with it, and to dry you out, but the best thing you can do for yourself is to drink juice, get plenty of rest, and take some aspirin for the achy feeling." He scribbled two prescriptions and handed them to her.

"How long does this bug last?" she asked.

"Oh, three or four days. Had it myself a few weeks ago. Not much you can do about it, but these should minimize the symptoms and make you more comfortable. You can fill your prescriptions downstairs."

Denney stopped on the stone steps of the Health Services Building to swallow the first round of both medications. She grimaced at the sour taste the pills left in her mouth. Sneezing again, she reached into her coat pocket, hoping she still had an unused tissue. She made a mental note to stop at the store on the way home to pick up another box or two of tissue.

Maybe, Denney thought, when she did get around to writing her paper, she could sneeze all over it and give Dr. Harris back the virus. She was pretty sure she had read somewhere that viruses last for hours on objects like doorknobs. Maybe paper was the same. At this politically incorrect thought, Denney chuckled, remembering how, as a child, she believed the only way to get rid of a cold was to give it to somebody else. To this day, Denney's mother swore that Denney had never brought home a cold she hadn't managed to pass on to at least one member of the family, usually her mother.

As Denney passed The Jugg, her eyes were drawn to an inviting "Hot Soup for Cold Days" sign recently placed in The Jugg's front plate glass window. Soup sounded good to Denney. She went inside to get a take-out order to ease her throat.

Kellie was waiting on a table at the far side of the restaurant. Seeing Denney, she waved. Denney nodded at her, but then turned to give her order to Pete at the counter. "Chicken noodle soup," he repeated.

"That's right. To go, please," she said, turning her head as she sneezed again.

"Sounds like you've got that bug your friend here had," Pete observed as Denney faced him again to pay for her soup.

"Yes, I think it finally got me. It seems to be making the rounds at the sorority house," Denney replied.

"You better keep your distance from her," Pete told Kellie as she came up behind him at the counter. Kellie made a little face and rolled her eyes as Pete walked back towards the kitchen to get the soup. Denney croaked a hello.

"You sound terrible," Kellie said. "How do you feel?"

"Not much better than I sound. I just came from Health Services. Hopefully the stuff they gave me will kick in soon. In the meantime, you really better not get too close. You wouldn't want a relapse," she said loudly, as Pete came back into earshot with the take-out carton. He handed the container to Kellie to ring up, and then, still watching them, began to clear a place setting a few feet down the counter. Picking up the dirty dishes, he disappeared through the swinging door into the kitchen. Kellie handed the soup to Denney.

"Relapse? I don't get it."

"The bug Harris had was the only thing I could think of when you called Pete the other day."

"You were here?"

"At the counter. I think I better get out of here before I really do pass this blasted thing on to you or somebody else." Denney turned her head quickly as she unsuccessfully tried to stifle another sneeze. Juggling the soup container, she left the restaurant. She really did have an urge to call her mother.

# TWENTY-TWO

*Monday, December 6, 1971*

ENTERING HER SORORITY room, Denney noticed her answering machine light blinking. Ignoring it, she put the soup container on her desk and took off her coat. Rather than hanging it up, she threw it on the chair on top of the gray suit that Kellie had returned. In the rush of things, Denney had yet to take it to the cleaners. She picked up the hot pot from the bookshelf and poured the soup into it. The newspaper was still on the shelf, but she ignored it. Instead, as she waited for her soup to warm, Denney dialed her mother.

The phone was answered by the prerecorded message that she had taped the last time she was home. Leaving her mother a quick hello message, she hung up. The red blinking light again caught her eye so she reached over and punched the playback button. The first two calls had been hang-ups. Marta had left a message confirming that the funeral would be the next day at ten. She asked Denney to call her back tonight if she still wanted a ride. The fourth missed call had been her mother inquiring whether she was studying too hard to pick up a telephone. Somewhat impatient with her mother's attempt at a guilt trip, Denney reached down to unplug the hot pot as the next message began. Recognizing Bill's voice, Denney's mood brightened.

"Hey, Denney," he said. "I've been trying to get you

all morning. We don't have class today, but when you get this message, please give me a call. I'd like to bring Suzanne by tomorrow tonight. Maybe about seven? I thought we could compare notes. You know, brainstorm about last night. Anyway, give me a call when you get this message."

Denney obediently called Bill back. She was about to hang up after the fifth ring when his answering machine intercepted the call. Rather than hanging up, Denney tried to sound somewhat nonchalant as she left a message telling Bill she was feeling a little under the weather, so perhaps sometime later in the week would be better for the three of them to get together. She hung up the phone satisfied with her message but knowing one thing for sure: she had no intention of ever brainstorming with Bill or Suzanne Harris.

# TWENTY-THREE

*Tuesday, December 7, 1971*

DENNEY WAS RUNNING late. Marta and the dorm crew would be at Sorosis any minute, and she still wasn't dressed for Helen's funeral. She had overslept. Then, realizing the suit that would have been perfect for the service was sitting in a heap on her chair, she had searched through her closet for something appropriate, that didn't have spots on it, before settling on a simple black suit with a gold blouse. When she was halfway dressed, her mother had called concerned about how bad Denney had sounded on her answering machine.

They talked for ten minutes before she finally convinced her mother that she had gone to Health Services and really was among the living. Her mother then took another ten minutes, despite Denney's telling her she was being picked up soon, to bring Denney up to date on the things happening at home. She only hung up when Denney insisted that her friends were outside honking for her. Denney felt guilty for rushing her mother off the phone and made a mental note to call her back for a longer conversation after the funeral.

The insistent buzzing of her personal code left no time to do anything except grab her jacket, purse, and an extra package of tissue. On the way out, she remembered that she had not taken her medicine this morning. Between the buzzer and actually feeling better, she decided not to waste time going back to her room. Taking her medicine would be just another thing for her after the funeral to-do list.

Marta was waiting in the lobby. Denney immediately smiled. Marta was one of those people who always made you feel good. Big-boned, with an informal sense of style, Marta's aw-shucks, farm-girl image worked to her advantage as the full-time resident manager of Michigan's largest dormitory. Most people thought they were dealing with a hayseed fresh off the truck before realizing that the dual psychology-business graduate had just outwitted them. Although there were other places that Marta could have worked for far higher wages, she enjoyed the campus niche she had carved out for herself.

Helen and Denney had each met Marta shortly after they moved into the dormitory. As the overall dormitory advisor, Marta essentially ran a small business entity. She was responsible for the budget, food, personnel, students, and facilities, but even with delegating the everyday functions to hall advisors in the nine Markley houses, she made it her business to get to know each dormitory resident. Marta had taken a special interest in Helen and Denney after purchasing their MMF doughnuts on the Diag from atop a table that looked strangely similar to one from her dining room.

When Helen became active in the Black Action Movement, Marta encouraged her involvement, but discreetly made sure to keep apprised of the extent of it. They had talked at length about the historical perspective of campus and administration reaction to prior protest activities that ranged from sit-ins and building takeovers to an unsuccessful attempt to sever the Hill from Central campus by blowing up the George Wheeler, nicknamed Ho Chi Minh, bridge. Marta had been the sounding board for Helen's involvement in the food strike. She also had run interference with the LS&A Dean and campus President to insure that Helen's nonviolent involvement did not result in expulsion. Later, she had championed her for a Blagdon House hall advisor job.

As friendly as Denney was with Helen, it was not until well after the BAM strike that Helen told Denney how much she had relied on Marta during that time period. It was Marta with whom Helen had felt the safest sharing her personal life. Marta knew that even with free room and board, Helen's father still worked two jobs, while her mother had a day job and took in sewing on the side, in the hope of obtaining college educations for their three children. It was to Marta that Helen came when her father had called incensed after reading a quote, attributed to her as one of the leaders of the BAM strike, in the Detroit Free Press. Marta had let her talk until Helen had realized that her father was petrified that Michigan would kick her out of school. Helen also had used Marta as her confidant during the time after the strike was over, when her relationship with her father remained rocky because he still clung to his anger that she had almost thrown her chance at a college education away by letting her heart overrule her mind.

"Thanks for including me today," Denney told Marta. "To tell you the truth, I'm glad to be going with a group rather than alone. Who is in the car?" she asked, as they walked down the steps.

"The other Blagdon House advisors—June, Hilary, and Tanya."

The ride to the Detroit church went quickly. Marta broke the ice by telling a humorous story about Helen. Soon, all five women were sharing personal memories

of their beloved friend and their bitterness at the trag-
edy of her death.

The church proved to be a small white clapboard
building in the middle of a somewhat run-down residen-
tial neighborhood. Although the building and the small
plot of land around it were well kept, many of the houses
on the street were in need of paint. Inside the chapel,
the only ornamentation contrasting with the stark white
walls was a huge cross that rose from the altar. Helen's
casket was nestled at the foot of the cross. Her parents
were standing to the side of the casket as people came
up to pay their respects. Next to them, sharing the same
well-chiseled features that Helen had had, were a girl of
about fifteen and a slightly younger boy.

The Blagdon bunch joined the line of people waiting to speak to Helen's family, but Denney decided to
first detour to the restroom to blow her nose in a more
private setting. She was taken aback to see Kellie in the
ladies lounge checking her lipstick in the mirror. Kellie
was wearing the still uncleaned suit Denney had thought
of wearing today. "What are you doing here?" Denney
sputtered. "You hardly knew Helen."

"What are you doing here?" Kellie countered. "I
thought you were sick so I came for you."

"Excuse me? By the way, I'm beginning to think
you're getting more use out of that suit than I am."

"I am."

"At least you're honest. You still haven't told me why
you're here."

"I really did come for you. Ferguson came into The
Jugg while I was working this morning and sat at the
counter. He told Pete and me he was driving some department members to the funeral today. It dawned on me

that you might be too sick to go so I asked if there was room in the car for me."

"After everything you told me about him, you had the audacity to ask for a ride? I can't believe that you would ride with him under any circumstances."

"Denney, he already had told me he was driving Mrs. Henderson, Professor Willoughby, and Mr. Godbolt. I figured with them in the car, what could happen except that I might pick up some more behind the scenes dirt for you. Look, I weighed wanting to come for Helen and you against the fact that he was my only means to get to here. It seemed more important to come than to worry about spending two hours in the car with him and three other people. You know, in all the mystery books I've ever read, the person who did it comes to the funeral."

"But those are fiction books," Denney protested.

"Maybe, but you never know. I almost didn't make it though. After my shift, I barely had time to get back to the sorority house to borrow your suit again before I had to be at Dr. Ferguson's office. As chairman of the English department, he felt an obligation, on behalf of the University, to be one of the first mourners here to express his condolences to Helen's parents. You know what's funny?" Kellie didn't wait for Denney to answer. "He got us here so early that we beat the family to the chapel. They just arrived a few minutes ago." She snapped her lipstick shut and dropped it back in her pocketbook. "Guess I better get back out there if I'm going to see anything that might be suspicious. Coming?" Starting towards the door, she paused and glanced back over her shoulder at Denney.

"In a moment. You keep your eyes open for me." After Kellie left the lounge, Denney went back into the stalls and pulled off a long strip of toilet paper. Gently, she blew her nose. Maybe, she thought, Kellie had a point.

She might see something that would help Denney figure
out why Helen was dead.

After checking her face in the mirror, Denney brushed
her hair back with her hand and went to pay her respects
to the Manchesters. Walking through the chapel towards
the casket, she saw that Marta and the other Blagdon advisors were already seated. Marta pointed towards her
pew to show Denney that she was saving a seat for her.
Denney acknowledged Marta before making her way
closer to the stalled makeshift receiving line. She slid into
a space near Kellie, just behind Willoughby and Godbolt.
Looking to the front of the line, she could see that the
delay was being caused by Dr. Ferguson and Mrs. Henderson monopolizing the family members.

Listening to bits and pieces of their conversation, Denney heard Dr. Ferguson saying to Mr. Manchester that
Helen had been a true delight as a student; that she had
the makings of a great scholar. At the same time, Mrs.
Henderson was grabbing Helen's mother's hands in hers.
Holding on tightly, she said, "Just knowing how devastat-
ing it is to me to have lost such a good friend as Helen,
I can't begin to imagine how terrible it must be for you
to have lost Helen."

"Thank you, Ms.—" Helen's mother began, obviously
unsure of who she was speaking with as she gracefully
extricated her hands.

"Henderson, Brenda Henderson. I'm sure Helen spoke
of me. She was a true friend. We worked together on the
Middle English Dictionary and shared many pleasant
times in the department."

Mrs. Manchester wrinkled her brow. "I'm afraid…."

"Oh, Helen technically worked as Professor Willoughby's research assistant, but we still had to collaborate
fairly often," Mrs. Henderson explained. "Let me tell

you, your daughter was the backbone of Professor Willoughby's work this year," she said, staring meaningfully at Dr. Ferguson, who was now listening. "She was the basis for anything Willoughby achieved this year."

"That she was," Dr. Ferguson concurred, as he stepped closer to Mrs. Henderson. He pressed his hand on her elbow to guide her forward. She didn't move. "Helen would have made a great addition to our staff, just like Mrs. Henderson here. We've always tried to find a place for our best and brightest." He looked behind him at the people waiting to pay their respects. "We better move along. We're holding up the line."

With a final look at the casket, Dr. Ferguson escorted Mrs. Henderson to a seat. Willoughby and Godbolt immediately approached the Manchesters and made perfunctory remarks about what a talented and wonderful person Helen had been. Kellie and Denney stepped forward next. Mrs. Manchester hugged Denney. "I'm so glad you were able to come, Denney. Helen spoke of you often. You truly had a gift for making her laugh." Thanking her for her kind words, Denney introduced Kellie to Mrs. Manchester and the rest of Helen's family.

As the two turned from the casket, they realized the pews behind them were almost filled to capacity. Kellie grabbed a seat in the row behind the Michigan staff members while Denney squeezed into the space that Marta had saved for her. Settling in, Denney's eye was caught by movement in the rear of the chapel. A cluster of people, having opted to stand for the service near the church's back entry, were being guided towards the side aisles so that the main aisle would not be blocked.

Denney saw Bill and Dr. Harris being ushered to the side where the English faculty members were sitting. For a moment, Denney stared at them in amazement.

She could not believe Bill would bring Suzanne Harris to the funeral or, for that matter, that Dr. Harris would have the balls to attend.

As the two walked by Dr. Ferguson, he reached into the aisle and tapped Bill's arm. When Bill turned towards him in response, both Dr. Ferguson and Mrs. Henderson leaned forward to talk to him. Denney couldn't hear what they were saying, but she hoped Dr. Ferguson and Mrs. Henderson were commenting on the inappropriateness of bringing Dr. Harris to Helen's funeral; but, after a brief exchange, during which nobody looked particularly distressed, Bill and Dr. Harris moved on.

Marta took in the stare that Denney was giving Dr. Harris, who was now deep in conversation with Mrs. Manchester. She broke Denney's concentration by whispering, "Put yourself in her shoes. She came to say goodbye to a friend."

"But…" Denney began.

"But," Marta interrupted, "assuming guilt and being quick to punish, may make you miss something." Denney could not believe this. It seemed as though Marta was defending Dr. Harris. "You know," Marta said, "maybe we should pick up a box of doughnuts on our way back to Ann Arbor."

# TWENTY-FOUR

*Tuesday, December 7, 1971*

WITH WAVES OF farewell, and an admonishment to feel better soon, the Blagdon girls dropped Denney back at the sorority after the funeral. The first thing Denney did once she reached her room was to take the medicine she had forgotten to take that morning; then, she called her mother. Denney hung up after half an hour of assuaging her guilt. She still felt unsettled, but decided she better start writing her poetry paper.

By the time Kellie stuck her head in a couple of hours later to return the floating suit, she found Denney, tissue box at her side, typing diligently. "How are you feeling?"

"Almost human. The medicine they gave me at Health Service really seems to be working."

"Well, I'm going to grab a quick nap, but I thought I would see if you need anything."

"No, thanks. I'm on a roll right now on my paper. Hopefully, by the time you finish your nap, I'll be finished with my draft."

"One of the few times I'm ahead of you. I wrote my paper the other day. So, I really have time to take a nap. See you later."

Denney returned her attention to flipping through the books that lay open around her. She had marked different pages in each of them so that she could easily pick and choose from the thoughts of different commentators for inclusion in her own critique. Her greatest difficulty was summarizing their ideas to fit on only two pages.

As she opened one of the books that she had previously bookmarked, her right arm shot up above her head. Startled, she reached up with her left hand and pulled it down. Her right arm was tingling. Deciding that perhaps she had dosed off and dreamt that her arm didn't want to be part of anything that might resemble plagiarism, Denney opted to take a break. Perhaps walking down the hall to the bathroom and splashing some water on her face would wake her up.

She stumbled as she stood up, but the sensation of being off balance quickly passed. In the ladies room, Denney washed and dried her face. She peered at her reflection in the mirror. The mirrored image seemed lopsided. She tried to straighten up, but still looked like she was listing to the left. Denney stared at herself in the mirror and then said: "Ah, this is how the hunchback of Notre Dame must have felt when he looked at his hump."

"No, don't be silly," another voice in her head chided. "This is how Dr. Jekyll and Mr. Hyde began."

Deciding that she really was standing normally and that holding discussions with herself in the bathroom mirror was not going to get her paper finished, Denney started back to her bedroom. She had taken just a few steps down the hall, when the fire door of the main staircase opened and Marilyn yelled: "Man on the floor. Man on the floor." Without looking to see if the hallway was clear, Marilyn waved for her parents to follow her. As Marilyn's mother and father were turning into the part of the hallway where Denney stood, Denney felt her arm begin inching upwards again.

She grabbed her arm with her left hand and forced

her right hand behind her neck. She leaned on the wall for balance, trying to look friendly as Marilyn's parents passed her. Almost as an afterthought, Marilyn intoned, "This is Denney Silber, Mom and Dad. The one I told you about." With matching nods of acknowledgement, Marilyn's parents quickly followed their daughter to the third floor. Once the stairwell door closed, the thought flashed through Denney's mind that she couldn't decide if they were mommy and poppy dearest or just an extension of the three bears.

Denney relaxed. Deciding that she was just being dramatic, she resumed working on her paper. She was so absorbed in juggling the ideas from the books with what she was typing on her paper, that she didn't hear Ana as she poked her head into Denney's room.

"How's the patient?" Ana asked. "Do you feel like coming down to dinner or would you like me to bring you something?"

"Is it dinnertime already? I'm not even hungry. I think I'll just work on my paper and pass on coming down tonight. Oh, and Ana, I'll get you a new bottle of aspirin when I'm out tomorrow. With the funeral and this paper, I never got to the store today."

"No rush. If there is anything good downstairs, I'll bring you a plate."

"Thanks, but don't bother. I really don't have much of an appetite."

After Ana left, Denney continued working on her paper. She was just putting the finishing touches on it when Ana and Kellie appeared at her door again. "She insisted that in order for you to get well, you need to eat healthy," Kellie said, pointing at the cooked carrots and other vegetables on the plate that Ana held, "but I fig-

ured you needed some of the good stuff." Kellie flipped
a bowl of vanilla ice cream out from behind her back.

"I'm most appreciative to both of you," Denney said,
reaching for the ice cream. Her right hand grasped the
ice cream dish, but her arm jerked again. The dish went
flying across the room, landing with a thud upside down
in the middle of the shag carpet. "Oh, I'm so sorry," Denney muttered as she rose to clean up the mess.

"Denney, are you all right?" Ana asked, putting the
food plate on the desk.

"Fine. My hand slipped." It dawned on her that her
right arm still was extended above her head. Using her
left hand, she started to pull on the right one, but yielded
when Kellie gently took her shoulder and, avoiding the
puddling ice cream, guided her to a sitting position on
her bed.

"I think we better get you back to Health Services,"
Kellie said with a glance at Ana. Without saying anything, Ana left the room. "Where are your sneakers?"

"Over there, but I don't need to go to Health Services.
I'm fine. See," she said, looking at her two hands that
now lay in her lap. "Really, I'm fine. Where did Ana go?"

"Humor us. We'll feel better if you see somebody."

"I'm fine. My hand slipped," Denney said shaking
Kellie's hand off her shoulder as she grabbed a towel
lying on the bed. "I need to clean this mess up." As Denney bent to wipe the ice cream up, she put her left hand on
the floor to steady herself. Kellie caught her as she began
to sway. Taking the towel from Denney, Kellie helped
her back to the bed. Without releasing her grasp, Kellie
used her leg to kick the sneakers closer to Denney. "Put
your sneakers on," she ordered, as Ana returned with car
keys and her pocketbook.

"Whose keys are those?" Denney asked, as she pushed her feet into her sneakers without opening the laces.

"Housemother's."

"Oh, no," groaned Denney.

"Is something hurting?" Ana asked with a look of concern.

"I keep telling you, and the Marquis de Sade here, that I'm fine. Within an hour, though, everybody is going to know about this wild-goose chase you are dragging me on."

"That's okay. It will make you a more sympathetic character instead of a grouch." Ana handed Denney her coat. They left Kellie cleaning up the ice cream.

# TWENTY-FIVE

*Tuesday Night, December 7, 1971*

ANA TRIED TO shield Denney from the cold wind as they stood outside Health Services' emergency entrance. She repeatedly pressed the squawk box buzzer. "Somebody is coming," Denney said. Through the double glass doors, the two girls could see the full-bodied figure of a female nurse walking deliberately towards them.

"That's enough bell ringing," said the nurse, as she swung open the door. "What seems to be the emergency?"

"She's been having some kind of reaction. Her arm."

"Nothing."

"Which is it?" asked the nurse, her eyes resting on Denney.

"My arm jerked up a few times, and well it scared us. I'm fine now."

"Let's make sure. Follow me." With the two in tow, she took them through another set of double doors into a small waiting room. "You can wait here," she said, indicating the chairs in the waiting room to Ana with a flick of her left hand. "You," she nodded to Denney, "come with me."

She led Denney through a wooden door adjacent to the receptionist window. Denney could see two feet in sneakers, with red socks, casually perched on the desk. Because the owner of the feet had his back to her, she was unable to see his face. From his lack of movement, she had a definite feeling that he was anything but energized.

The drill sergeant in white escorted Denney into an examination room. She handed her a paper gown and told her to strip down to her bra and panties. The nurse left the room to give Denney a chance to change in private.

Denney turned the gown back and forth trying to figure out whether it opened in back or in front. She finally put it on in the manner that she thought would be the least revealing and then carefully arranged herself and the gown on the examining table. Nobody seemed to be in much of a hurry to come so Denney guessed it was a good thing she wasn't dying. She had almost decided to move from the table to the chair in the corner, when, before she could reply to a knock at the door, it was flung open with a "Hello, I'm Dr. Oliver. What do we have here?"

"A would-be patient," Denney replied. Looking down at the red socks showing out from the gap between his sneakers and his green scrubs, Denney recognized the feet as having been the ones parked on the desk.

"I would hope so. That's the kind of business we're in. No patients, no business," he joked. Ignoring his stab at humor, Denney checked Dr. Oliver out. Taking her eyes from his feet, she followed the hem of the white lab coat he wore over his scrubs up to an unevenly cut head of dirty blond hair. Denney thought he looked more like a waiter than a doctor. In fact, the only thing that gave him any credibility as a doctor was the stethoscope carefully draped around his neck. "So, what seems to be the problem that couldn't wait until morning?"

"I picked up the bug that is going around. I actually came to Health Services to get something to knock it out."

"I see that," he said peering at her file. "And?"

"And, I was feeling a lot better, but a little while ago,

my arm jerked up a few times and I had this funny feeling that I was tilting to the side. When I dropped a bowl of ice cream, my friends thought I needed to come in."

"Well, your friends probably had the right idea. Dropping ice cream is a serious symptom. Better to be safe than sorry. Let's see what we can find." He began to examine her ears, throat, nose, and glands. After listening to her chest through his stethoscope, he observed that "other than still having that cold that brought you in yesterday, there doesn't seem to be anything out of the ordinary. Maybe you were feeling a little stressed or something?"

"Stressed? That's your diagnosis? Come on, Dr. Oliver, what college student isn't stressed? My arm didn't go up in the air because I'm stressed."

"Okay, so it isn't stress. Just thought I would mention it since I can't find anything else." Denney was about to retort that she doubted he would have mentioned stress to a male patient when he couldn't find anything to diagnose, but before she could say anything, Dr. Oliver was already in motion. "Take the medication we gave you, get plenty of rest, and this shall pass before you know it," he said flippantly. "When you get dressed, come out to the desk and pick up your checkout papers." Without giving Denney a chance to respond, he was out of the examination room.

Denney climbed off the examining table feeling somewhat embarrassed. She put her blouse and pants on and was slipping her arms into her jacket as she began walking down the hallway towards the receptionist desk. Reaching the counter where Dr. Oliver was handing papers to the nurse for what she presumed would be her checkout, she felt the strange sense of rigidness returning to her arm. She looked at the two of them. She could no more control her arm than the strange voice coming through her pursed lips: "It's happening again. Please, I don't usually talk like this."

Stepping around the seemingly frozen doctor, the nurse quickly moved to steady her. "Let me help you," the nurse said, pulling Denney's coat off as she guided her back into the exam room. Lying flat on the examining room table, Denney tried to calm herself by concentrating on what Dr. Oliver and the nurse were doing. She found she could only focus on one activity at a time. It was easier to follow the steps of the nurse putting a blood pressure cuff on her arm, taking her pulse, and unbuttoning her shirt, than to give in to the mounting panic she felt at the way her body was responding.

Denney tried to speak, but she could not seem to form the words that were running through her brain. And then everything was replaced by a warm sensation of yellow. Yellow daisies? Sunshine? Denney was conscious of movement and noise around her, but now it didn't seem important. Everything was so calm, and the light was inviting and safe. That was it, she felt safe. She couldn't see herself walking through the yellow, but just as she had had the earlier sensations of jerking, she knew she was moving in a floating relaxed manner greeting people and being greeted.

Grandma, grandpa, I've always wanted to meet you, she thought. She couldn't see their faces, but instinctively knew she could touch them in the whirl of yellow. She reached her right hand out to touch the warm swirling flood of light. And then it was over. The yellow was gone.

"That's more like it. I think you're out of the woods now," the nurse said as she gently patted Denney's hand. "You scared us for a few minutes there."

"You certainly did," Dr. Oliver agreed. Beads of sweat

were still apparent on his forehead as he dropped a syringe into a red toxic disposal can.

"What happened?" Denney asked. Or at least she thought she did, the words sounding soft and slurred in her ear.

"Take it easy. You had an autonomic reaction—probably to the Combid that they prescribed for you."

"But I only had two pills." She tried to hold up two fingers.

"Two too many. It was toxic for you." Seeing confusion on Denney's face, he explained further. "It caused involuntary spasms of your muscles."

"My arm?"

"Yeah, that's why your arm kept shooting up and why you were having trouble breathing." Denney didn't understand what he was talking about, but she was too tired to speak. "Your heart is a muscle, too. It's just a good thing you were here when you went into that last spasm. We had to give you a shot of Benadryl to relax your muscles."

"Oh," Denney shuddered. The nurse again placed her hand on Denney's arm. At her touch, Denney felt herself relaxing, but she noticed that she still had a tight sensation in the center of her right hand. She tried to flex the fingers, but wasn't sure if they actually were moving. Everything felt like it was in slow motion.

"Don't worry. With the dose of Benadryl we gave you, you should be fine, but really drowsy. It's going to take a while to sleep off the Benadryl's effects. For peace of mind, I'm going to admit you to the student infirmary so we can keep an eye on you. Now, if you don't need anything else," he said, "I'm going to change the orders I was writing up on you."

Once again, not giving her time to say anything else, he left the room. With effort, Denney turned her head for a better view of the nurse who was now disposing of a vial, towels, and gauze pads that had apparently fallen while they were taking care of her. Sensing Denney looking at her, the nurse stopped what she was doing and came closer to the gurney. "Let yourself go back to sleep," she said, patting her arm. "You'll feel a lot better. Everything really is okay now."

"Woozy," Denney whispered.

"That's to be expected. I get sleepy if I take one or two Benadryls over the counter, and we gave you a much higher dosage than that. Don't be surprised if once you get in your room, you sleep until sometime tomorrow."

"My friend?" Denney began.

"Still here. In fact, you've become quite popular. When I peeked out a few minutes ago to bring your friend up to date, I found she had been multiplying, like rabbits," the nurse quipped. "Tell you what, it's quiet here tonight. We'll let them all come back and visit with you while we're arranging for a bed. Now, why don't you rest for a few minutes while I get them?" Relieved, Denney closed her eyes.

"You certainly scared us," Ana said as she gently stroked Denney's hair. Whether it was Ana's voice or touch, Denney blinked her eyes open in startled recognition. She tried to tell Ana that there was nothing to worry about, but only a stifled yawn came out as she again closed her eyes. With her eyes shut, Denney had a feeling that her other senses were more heightened. She was conscious of movement around her, and of the smells of disinfectant mixing with whiffs of perfume, and, if she was correct, aftershave lotion. She tried to associate the information her senses was processing with who was in the room, but she felt confused. The soft touch on her hair was replaced for a moment with someone with a more overpowering scent. What was Kellie doing here, she thought. Straining to see, the image she perceived was Bill and Dr. Harris, but the voice that seemed to come from them was that of Kellie. "Girl, you certainly do things in a dramatic fashion," Kellie observed. "Now, you promise us, no more fun tonight. You just take it easy."

"Promise," Denney whispered as she stopped struggling to keep her eyes open. She barely heard Ana say she would bring her some clothes and toiletries in the morning.

# TWENTY-SIX

*Wednesday, December 8, 1971*

IT TOOK DENNEY a few seconds to remember that she was in the infirmary. She was in the bed closest to the door. The second bed was empty. She was unsure of how long she had slept. Noticing a control attached to her bed, she pushed the button marked with a lightbulb. A light behind the bed sputtered on allowing Denney to see the room in more detail.

It was fairly sparse. Two beds, two chairs, two bedside tables, and a wall clock were the basic décor. No television. Someone had tried to improve the hospital room's sterile atmosphere by hanging two still-life pictures across from the beds. Rather than being a cheerful addition to the room, the pictures accentuated its institutional nature. In fact, the sameness of the pictures made Denney feel like she was in a seedy motel room.

The clock behind Denney read 4:00, but with the blackout blinds drawn, she still wasn't quite sure if it was morning or afternoon. Although she could hear noises in the hall, she couldn't distinguish the sounds. Sitting up, she swung her legs over the edge of the bed. Still feeling groggy, she remembered that even though she normally never did it, it was supposed to be a good idea to sit a moment before standing up.

Before she could rise, the door to her room was pushed open by a nurse she did not recognize. "Hi, sleeping beauty," the nurse said as she thrust a thermometer into Denney's mouth and took her arm to check her pulse. "My name is Jill, and I'm your nurse for this shift. I see you've finally decided to rejoin the world of the living. How do you feel?"

"Awfully sleepy. I'm not even sure if it's morning or afternoon."

"With all the Benadryl they gave you, that's to be expected. It's Wednesday morning, about 4:15 a.m.," she said, glancing at her watch. "Anything tight or uncomfortable?"

"Basically, except for being sleepy, and my right hand tingling a little, I feel fine."

"Can you move your fingers?"

"Oh yeah, my hand works." Denney moved her hand so Jill could see it. "It just feels a little funny in the center of the palm. Maybe I clenched it a little too tight last night. I really do feel fine."

"That's good to hear. You certainly gave Dr. Oliver and your friends a scare. It was a good thing you were at the infirmary when your reaction became so severe. Now, why don't you rest a little more? I'll bring you a breakfast tray between five and six, and rounds should be about that time, too. Don't forget to tell the doctor about your hand. In the meantime, if you need anything else, just ring your buzzer."

"Thanks, Jill." After Jill left, Denney got up and opened the curtains. She looked out the window for a few minutes and then walked back to bed. She would have watched some television if the room had had a TV. Instead, she lay back down on the bed and stared at the two pictures across from her. They were even more obnoxious looking if one studied them carefully.

Denney still was contemplating the pictures when she

heard a knock at her door. Before she could call, "Come in," the door was opened by the young doctor she had seen downstairs. Looking at him framed in the doorway by the light of the hall, she decided he really was too young to be a doctor. Denney also observed that he was wearing the same clothing as the evening before, including the red socks. "Dr. Oliver?" Denney asked.

"Guilty. I didn't think after the excitement of last night you would remember my name." Denney didn't choose to enlighten him that Jill had just mentioned his name. "How do you feel?"

"Much better thank you. Isn't it a little early for rounds?"

"Well," he said sheepishly. "My shift is about over. I won't be the doctor making rounds, but with the kind of reaction you had, I just wanted to poke my head in. I checked on you earlier, but you were out cold. I asked Jill to buzz me when you woke up. She did, and since things are quiet downstairs, I thought I would wander up here."

Denney did not say anything, but she wondered about his concern. In her experience, most doctors would have washed their hands of a patient by now. "Jill's notes indicate you are having some trouble with your right hand," he said after consulting her chart. Placing the chart on the edge of her bed, he reached for her hand and began manipulating it.

"It just tingles a little. Nothing like last night. I really feel back to normal."

"They will want to keep an eye on this, but it should go away fairly quickly. You definitely look better today. In fact, you don't even look like you did last night."

"I don't?"

"No," he said quite seriously. "Your face and features were somewhat swollen and distorted. If I had ever seen you before, like I'm seeing you now, I would have known you were in distress."

"Dr. Oliver, I feel like you just slammed me. That's not very good bedside manner," she teased.

"I'm sorry. No offense meant," he stammered.

"None taken. I'm just grateful you were able to stop the reaction." She sensed that he felt uncomfortable. "Now, it's my turn to be sorry. I didn't mean to embarrass you. I really do appreciate you taking care of me last night."

"Look, I'd like to take full credit for helping you, but I really can't. We always kid that Nurse Stephenson is a drill sergeant, but she knows her stuff. Last night, once you started having the spasm reaction, it took me a minute to figure out what was going on. My only exposure to that kind of reaction, before seeing you, was in my textbooks. I academically knew what needed to be done, but I had to grab the reference book we keep at the desk to check the correct amount of medication to give you. I hate to confess that I still was looking up the protocol while Nurse Stephenson was pulling out the Benadryl and needle. Considering how quickly your breathing became labored, she saved valuable time having the Benadryl ready. She's the one you need to thank," he admitted.

The earnestness of his admission made Denney look at him in a new way. "At least you knew what needed to be done. I gather this doesn't happen often," she said, trying to make him feel more comfortable.

"Thank goodness, no. After we got you upstairs to the infirmary, I did a little research. If I'm right, you made medical history at the University of Michigan."

"I did?"

"Yup, second lowest dosage of that medication to cause a toxic reaction. For your own protection, you need to make sure you never take anything else in the Combid/Compazine family."

"I can assure you that is one family of drugs I will remember to avoid. I never want to go through that much fun again."

"Can't say I blame you, Ms. Silber."

"Denney," she corrected.

"As I was saying, Denney, as severe as your reaction was, you were lucky your friends brought you to Health Service."

"It scares me to think what might have happened if they hadn't made me come."

"It scares me, too. I've been thinking about it all night." Dr. Oliver looked straight at her. Seeing the circles around his eyes, she realized how frightened of this unknown reaction he must have been. Now, she understood the extra patient care. Denney instinctively reached out and touched his hand. His eyes followed to where their skin made contact.

"You did the right thing. Look, everything works," she said, squeezing his hand with her right hand. She removed her hand and waved it so he would not think she was being forward. "See," she said wriggling each finger, "the hand is fine. And now, if you see this reaction again, you'll always know how much Benadryl to use." He smiled. "Maybe I don't want to know this, but how long have you been practicing?"

"I finished an internship in May, and now I'm doing my residency at University Hospital. I moonlight at Health Services a few nights a month," he replied. "Since I've been moonlighting, the shifts have been fairly quiet; at least, until this one."

"Everybody needs some excitement occasionally,"

Denney noted. "You don't impress me as somebody who likes to be bored."

"I'm not. My specialization is going to be emergency medicine. Right now, I'm spending a lot more time in the emergency room than I am at home. Moonlighting for Health Services pays me rather well, and usually gives me the opportunity to catch up on my sleep. Speaking of which, I'm going to leave them an order to give you an oral dose of Benadryl."

"But I'm going home in a few hours," she protested. "Any more Benadryl will put me back in la-la land."

"It won't matter this morning. We're going to keep you another day until that tingling in your hand is completely gone. If everything is okay, the attending will release you in the morning."

"Dr. Oliver, I'm fine. I have a lot of things to do today so why don't you just skip the Benadryl. I want to go home as soon as it is daylight."

"You probably are fine now, but your body didn't think so just a few hours ago. Take the Benadryl and let everything go for today. It really is better to be safe than sorry."

Denney frowned. She didn't like that he seemed to be patronizing her. "I really don't appreciate your attitude. You're not the only one who can make an intelligent decision."

"I'm sure you normally can, but today, you need to listen to me and stay put." He stood up and picked up her chart.

"If I were you, I would rethink my manner of dealing with female patients. Your know-it-all attitude demonstrates a definite lack of bedside manner."

"Ms. Silber, I'm not trying to be charming."

"That's obvious."

"I'm just trying to practice good medicine," he continued. "I doubt you will have any more problems, but even after the first Benadryl shot, I wasn't convinced that the reaction wouldn't occur again when it wore off. That's why I left that tray over there." He pointed to a wrapped epinephrine syringe box sitting on a plastic tray on the far bedside table. Seeing the box on the table and realizing the fear that had prompted its presence left Denney without a retort. "I didn't want to have any delays if you had any more problems. So, if you don't mind, humor me for the last few minutes of my shift. I don't care what you do to the next guy, but I want to know that I left you having had proper medical attention." With that declaration, Dr. Oliver took her chart and abruptly left the room.

"You can't just walk out!"

As the door slammed, Denney punched her call button. A moment later, a voice came over the intercom: "Can I help you?"

"I want to see Dr. Oliver again," Denney shouted into the speaker.

"I'll tell your nurse."

Denney was still sitting on the bed fretting about Dr. Oliver when the door opened again. Before she could sarcastically suggest that knocking would be appropriate, she realized that the face peering around the door belonged to Ana.

"Hi," Ana said. "I brought you a few of your own things. I was going to leave them at the nurses' station, but the nurse was certain you were awake and thought you wouldn't mind my popping in." She put the large tote bag she was carrying on one of the chairs. "You look much better than last night." She pulled Denney's robe from the bag and lay it on the bottom of the bed. Reaching back into the bag, she took out Denney's purple furry slippers. She put them on the floor next to the bed. "How are you feeling?"

"Stir crazy and ready to go home," Denney replied, "but they won't let me until at least tomorrow. What are you doing here so early? This stuff could have waited."

"I know, but I was already out," she said, placing Denney's hairbrush on her nightstand. "A few of us are going out for a breakfast powwow this morning. I figured since I was getting a ride to breakfast, we could take a quick detour so I could drop this stuff off before we ate. Hospitals always start so early that I thought you might want your robe and personal things."

"I appreciate it. Thanks. What group are you meeting with this morning?" Denney was curious. She couldn't imagine how Ana could add one more thing to what she already did.

"A new group that won't be around long as it has a limited purpose. Changing to the more important subject, why are they keeping you?"

"I made the mistake of telling the nurse that I have a little tingling in my right hand and she dutifully reported it to the doctor. He went berserk when he found out. Now, they won't release me until they are sure the reaction has completely resolved." Ana laughed at the annoyed face Denney was making.

"I'm sure that won't take too long. You'll be back at the sorority in a day or so."

"You sound like Dr. Oliver."

"The cute guy from last night?"

"What do you see in him that is cute?" Denney asked, forgetting to complain about still being held captive.

"Denney, he was really nice last night. When he came out to explain to all of us what had happened and why he was admitting you for a day or two, we could tell how worried he was about you."

"I want to go home now," Denney repeated.

"Well, you can't," Ana said, reaching around Denney to straighten her pillow. "You're not coming back to the sorority, or going anywhere else for that matter, until you are 100 percent well. Get it through your head, this is one time you are going to do exactly what the doctors and nurses tell you."

"Yes, ma'am." She leaned back against the pillow. "Who all was up here last night? I must have been hallucinating. One minute I thought I was talking to you and the next minute I could have sworn that Bill and Dr. Harris were here."

"They were." Seeing Denney's perplexed expression, Ana continued. "Right after we left, they came by the sorority house."

Mockingly hitting her head, Denney exclaimed: "Bill must not have gotten my message responding to his message!" It was Ana's turn to look confused. "Bill left me a phone message Monday saying he wanted to bring Dr. Harris over to the sorority yesterday around seven," Denney explained. "When I got his message, I called him back and left a message on his machine telling him I wasn't feeling well and that it would be better if we postponed getting together until later in the week. To be honest, I thought it would be better if we never got together."

"Well, they showed up at seven. When you didn't answer your page, Bill had them buzz Kellie. She filled them in on what had happened and that you were at Health Services. Because I hadn't called Kellie yet, they figured something must be wrong so they came over here to check things out for themselves. You were going in and out of the twilight zone when they let us see you. I'm amazed you remember anything from last night."

"Not much. It's a swirl of images and colors, especially yellow and green."

"You were really out of it," Ana observed.

"It was weird," Denney acknowledged. "I felt like I was in the room, seeing and knowing everything, and yet I wasn't there."

"Don't let it worry you. You're all right now." She reached behind Denney for the pillow she had just straightened and made a pretense of fluffing it before taking aim and hitting Denney with it. Denney ducked and then jumped from the bed. She grabbed the pillow from the extra bed. In a moment, the two were engaged in a full fledged pillow fight.

"What's going on in here?" Jill asked, as she came in carrying a fresh pitcher of water and a small medicine cup. "You belong in bed, young lady," she said sternly as she placed the pitcher on the side table. Pouring water into the pink plastic cup that matched the pitcher, she handed the drink and the pills to Denney. Denney couldn't look at Ana, now busily arranging the pillow on the spare bed.

"I better run before they think I've checked in here, too. Do you need anything else before I leave?" Ana asked.

"No, but thanks for coming by with my stuff. I guess I'm here for awhile," she said, with a look at Jill, who nodded. "At least, I'm guaranteed to catch up on my sleep."

# TWENTY-SEVEN

*Wednesday, December 8, 1971*

STILL AMUSED BY Ana's visit, Denney fell into a drugged sleep, oblivious to the infirmary sounds, including Jill periodically coming into the room to check on her. It was a smell that finally caused her to stir. With her eyes still closed, the sweet fragrance seemed familiar. For some reason, it made her think of Helen. Without being fully awake, she turned her head towards the other bedside table and called out: "Helen?"

There was no response, but a sense of movement brought Denney further out of her stupor. Trying to force her eyes to focus, she glimpsed something white. Before she could be certain what it was, her vision was blocked by an object being pushed against her face. She panicked at the feeling of being unable to catch her breath even as she realized a pillow was what was being used to hold her down. As she tried to turn away from her attacker, she heard something fall to the floor. For a moment the pressure lessened, but she was unable to break free.

She felt a sharp pain in her side. It dawned on her that she had rolled onto the nurse call button. She slid her fingers over the handset, hoping to find the button. Hearing a soft ding, she prayed that she had pushed it hard enough that someone would respond.

As a voice coming from the wall cheerfully asked, "May I help you?" the person gave one more shove and then fled the room. Throwing the pillow off her face, Denney caught a glimpse of white, but she couldn't make out if it was a coat, a hand, or even a glove. As Denney started towards the door, the wall voice repeated, "May I help you?"

"Please help me! Somebody just tried to kill me!"

"I'll tell your nurse," the voice calmly responded. Too soon for it to be the nurse, the door opened and Dr. Harris came in. Frightened, Denney looked around the room wildly, and then grabbed the water pitcher from the nightstand.

"Don't come near me," Denney shouted brandishing the water pitcher. Dr. Harris came closer to the bed. Denney yelled, "I'm warning you. Don't take another step!" Not really stepping towards the bed, Dr. Harris leaned down to pick up the pillow that was on the floor. As she bent forward, Denney heaved the pitcher at her. It missed, splattering water near the door just as Bill and Ana followed Kellie and Jill into the room.

"What's going on?" the nurse demanded.

"Somebody just tried to kill me! Please, call the police," Denney begged. No one moved despite Denney's obviously agitated state. Denney began to cry. "Please," she implored, staring at Bill. He stepped around the crowd, sat down on the bed and enveloped her in his arms.

"You're shaking," he said.

"Somebody just tried to kill me," she repeated, looking menacingly at Dr. Harris.

"What do you mean?" Bill gently asked.

"I was sleeping, and something woke me up."

"It must have been something loud," Jill said. "For the past few hours, I've been in and out and you never budged."

"No, it wasn't noise that woke me, or if it did, that wasn't what I was conscious of. It was a smell; a feeling. You'll think I'm crazy, but it was the perfume scent I associate with Helen. I think I even called out her name before I quite woke up." Seeing the concern on her friends' faces, Denney quickly assured them, "Don't worry, I'm not going crazy. Once I was more awake, I knew that Helen being here wasn't possible, that I had to have been dreaming, but I realized there was someone in my room."

"Did you see the person?" Bill queried.

"No, I wasn't quite focusing yet when I turned my head towards the sound. I glimpsed something white and the end of something plastic as my face was covered. We struggled, and I heard something fall, but I never could get out from the under the pillow enough to see who was holding me down."

"Is this what fell?" Dr. Harris bent down and picked up a plastic syringe that was partially under the bed.

"Don't touch that," Kellie admonished. "It probably has fingerprints. Here, put it in here," she said as she grabbed the unused pink spittoon dish that had come with the water glass and pitcher. Dr. Harris dropped the syringe into the dish, and Kellie put it back on the table.

"Maybe you were dreaming?" Jill ventured. "You don't seem to have much tolerance for Benadryl."

"Trust me, I didn't imagine somebody coming after me pushing a pillow down on my face."

"I know you didn't," Bill said, holding her close. "I think we better call security and maybe Sergeant Rutledge."

"Rutledge?" Kellie asked. "Why not just campus security?"

"Because, if somebody was trying to hurt Denney,

it really is quite a coincidence or the odds are that it is related to Helen's murder. In that case, this is Sergeant Rutledge's jurisdiction. Campus security will defer to him. With the way he feels about all of us after the other night, I think it would be the better part of valor for us to include him at this point. That way, he can't say we tried hiding anything."

# TWENTY-EIGHT

*Wednesday, December 8, 1971*

SERGEANT RUTLEDGE DID not seem particularly pleased to see the crew in Denney's room. Reviewing his notes after she finished telling what had happened, his face took on a dubious look. "So, if I got this right, you were asleep. Somebody attacked you. You saw something white that might have been a syringe or might have been a hand, but you never saw if the hand belonged to a man, woman, or what?"

"Not what. A person pushed a pillow into my face before I knew what was happening."

"Okay, and then you struggled, but during the entire encounter you never once turned your head to a position that let you see out from under the pillow."

"I couldn't. My head was pinned. Everything was happening too quickly," Denney explained.

"Did you put up any kind of fight before you finally punched your emergency call button?" Ignoring Denney nodding in the affirmative, the sergeant continued speaking. "And you say the voice coming over the loudspeaker was enough to scare your attacker off?"

"I think so."

"You make it sound preposterous," Bill bristled. "Sergeant Rutledge, she's telling you the truth."

"I'm not disputing that, Mr. Smythe. I'm just repeating what she told me. If you want to draw conclusions, you're free to do so. Now, let me see if I got the rest of this right. Except for you," he said nodding towards Jill, "the rest of you were together. And I assume you can vouch for each other for this morning?"

"She wasn't with us," Kellie said, pointing at Dr. Harris, "but the rest of us went to breakfast and came back here to surprise Denney."

"So the three of you were at the nurses' station, but you," he looked at Dr. Harris, "came into Ms. Silber's room without them?"

"That's right," Dr. Harris said softly, but Jill disagreed. "She came in alone. These two were talking with me just before I got the relayed message," she said, flipping her hand towards Bill and Ana, "but she caught up to us as we were coming into the room."

Rutledge looked at Kellie and waited expectantly. "I went to the bathroom. My hands were dirty," she explained.

"Did you see anybody in the bathroom?" Sergeant Rutledge asked.

"It's a one seater. I didn't see anybody in it, and I doubt anybody saw me in it, either. What about the syringe that was on the floor?" Kellie asked reaching for the spittoon dish. She held it out towards Sergeant Rutledge.

"What about it?" Rutledge asked.

"Somebody tampered with it," Denney said. "It was in its box on that table." She pointed to the nightstand on the far side of the room. "Dr. Oliver left it here last night in case I needed another shot. Maybe it has some fingerprints on it?"

Sergeant Rutledge looked at Dr. Harris as he bagged the syringe. "I doubt we can get anything off of this surface but if we do, you've just given all of us a logical explanation for the presence of your fingerprints on it."

Dr. Harris didn't react. He turned back towards Denney. "Maybe Dr. Oliver left the syringe ready in case he needed it?"

"No, it was wrapped in its box," Denney assured him.

"We'll check with him. You yourself said you've been sleeping most of the time since last night. You probably just didn't realize he left it open."

"I didn't realize it was open because it was closed."

"And you also thought Helen was here," Sergeant Rutledge reminded her.

# TWENTY-NINE

*Wednesday, December 8, 1971*

DENNEY STILL WAS furious with Sergeant Rutledge's comments as she walked into her sorority room. Having watched Denney divert her anger into an uncompromising demand to be released against medical advice from the infirmary, Bill stood quietly in her doorway holding her bag. When they had arrived at the sorority house, Ana and Kellie had thought it best to give Denney a little time to decompress. Hoping that Bill would be a calming influence, they took Dr. Harris up to their room. Now, alone with Denney, Bill was uncertain what to say lest she turn on him.

Seeing how awkward Bill seemed, Denney almost laughed. "You can come all the way in," Denney invited. "I'm not going to bite your head off." She sat down on her bed, taking in the fact that Ana or Kellie had straightened up by making a few piles of the things she had left thrown on her floor and bed.

"I wasn't quite sure," Bill responded, forcing a laugh that he stifled when Denney stared at him. Thinking it best not to say anything more, Bill put Denney's things down beside the chair nearest the door, placed his keys on her dresser, and then, pushing the gray suit aside, sat down on the chair.

"Well?" she demanded.

"Well, what?"

"You obviously want to say something. What is it?"

"Nothing really. I just hate to see you so upset."

"I'm not upset. I'm mad. In fact, I'm furious at Rutledge. He is a pompous fool. He didn't believe me so I doubt he will try to do anything about finding the person who attacked me. I don't know if it gets me madder that the bad guy will get away or that Sergeant Rutledge didn't believe me."

"Well, look at it from his perspective," Bill urged. "The nurse told Rutledge you had been out of it almost since you arrived. You admitted that you were in a fairly deep sleep when somebody supposedly attacked you. You even thought it was a dream at first, and you told him you were too groggy to respond quickly. Denney, by the time Sergeant Rutledge got there, you were still pretty foggy from the medication. He wouldn't have been doing his job if he didn't consider the possibility you might have imagined everything."

"Is that what you think, too? Maybe I was groggy or foggy or just downright out of it? I know exactly what happened to me! I assure you that I didn't image that pillow being pushed down on my face," she snapped.

"Hey, come on. I'm on your side. I know you believe somebody stuffed a pillow in your face, but look at it from his viewpoint. You were the only patient in the infirmary; there was only one nurse on duty; and, even though she was at the desk alone, she can account for what she and everybody else on the floor were doing for that time period."

"We may have been the only two people officially on that floor, but we were not the only two people in the building," Denney argued. "Four of you came on the floor, and there would have been at least one doctor and nurse on call downstairs. There also could have been

patients in the examining rooms, and other people in
the waiting room or hallway. Who did you see when you
came in? Did you come through the main door or did you
use your specialty, one of the steam tunnel entrances?"

"There may have been lots of people in the building,
but the nurse swore she didn't see anybody on your floor
until Suzanne got there and asked for your room."

"That doesn't mean anything. Maybe she was looking in a different direction or was getting water or something. Maybe she was in my room when the person came
on the floor."

"Doubtful," he replied. "She distinctly remembered
talking to Suzanne when she got off the elevator, and
she remembers her going into your room. She swears the
next person off the elevator was Kellie, followed a few
minutes later by Ana and me."

"She could be mistaken. Maybe my assailant used the
stairs," Denney stubbornly argued. "Bill, why didn't the
four of you just come up to my room together?"

"Because we didn't come together. Ana, Kellie, and
I ran errands and had breakfast. We dropped Kellie off
while Ana and I went to park. It was just coincidence
that Suzanne came over to see you at the same time we
did. You know, she wanted to meet with you for an idea
sharing session. She seems to think one of us might have
seen something at school, or even at the funeral, that will
help put Helen's murder into perspective."

Bill's mention of Helen's death diverted her attention.
Sitting on the edge of the bed across the room from Bill,
she looked at him, now eager to brainstorm. Before anything more could be said, Ana stuck her head into the
room. Quickly determining that some type of truce was
in effect, she looked back over her shoulder and waved

her hand. Immediately, Dr. Harris and Kellie joined her in the doorway.

The sight of the three of them crammed into the doorway made Denney and Bill burst out laughing. "What were you," Bill asked Ana, "the advance unit?" Bill moved over to sit on the bed with Denney to give the others more space in the cramped room.

"You might say that," she replied. "Thought I better make certain there was no friendly fire to contend with. Is there?"

"No," said Denney. "Bill and I were just going to brainstorm about Helen's death and the funeral."

"It was certainly a well-attended funeral," Kellie noted.

"I knew she was popular, but I didn't realize how many people's lives she touched."

"That she did. And she would have made such a difference. She could have done so much more." Dr. Harris turned from them to stare out the window. Somewhat shocked at her vehemence, the other four stared at her. Not taken aback, even though tears dotted her cheeks, Dr. Harris continued talking in the direction of the window about what Helen had hoped to achieve.

Neither Denney nor Bill did anything to break her train of thought. Kellie awkwardly distanced herself from the group by straightening the jacket of the gray suit that Bill had pushed aside on the chair. She kept her face averted from Dr. Harris. Only Ana seemed motivated to movement by the emotion of the moment.

Without saying anything, she moved towards Dr. Harris and easily rested her hand on the older woman's arm. It was as if Ana's touch worked to turn off a light switch. Dr. Harris stopped talking in mid-sentence and went from watching the cars passing on Washtenaw Avenue to collapsing in Ana's arms. Denney was not quite sure what had happened, but one minute, Ana and Harris had been two separate entities; now, the two stood together crying softly.

"Come on you two, cut it out," Denney urged. "You've even got Kellie tearing up." She pointed at Kellie who was staring intently at the subtle plaid in the jacket. "If all of you don't stop, I'm going to lose it, too. Poor Bill will drown in our tears. Please, one of you, tell me about the day that I pretty well managed to sleep away."

"The weather was good," Ana said weakly.

Still emotionally wound up, Dr. Harris looked at them, and asked: "How can you be so trite? Talking about the weather and avoiding the real issue?"

"The real issue?" Denney asked politely.

"The issue of who killed Helen. No matter what you think, Denney, I didn't. So, we need to figure out who did." As Denney began to respond, her words were drowned out by the sound of sirens.

"Fire!" somebody yelled. From above them, they could hear the sound of people running down the third floor stairwell. "Fire! The Phi Delt house is on fire!"

# THIRTY

*Wednesday, December 8, 1971*

WHEN THE GROUP from Denney's bedroom reached the street, they saw people from the other nearby sorority and fraternity houses running towards the Phi Delt house. Sirens were blaring as more fire trucks and police cars reached the scene. Already, police officers were working to control the gathering crowd.

From the sidewalk, flames could be seen coming out of the upper story windows. A loud crashing noise made Denney look just in time to see a stereo system falling through the broken glass from a third story room. Immediately, firemen turned hoses on the broken window through which Denney could now make out the figure of a young man. "That's near the meeting room," Bill cried, as he began running towards the building.

"Bill!" Denney shouted, losing sight of him as he pushed through the crowd towards the back of the building. In addition to the hoses trained on the window area, Denney realized that the nearest fire truck had begun swinging its sectional ladder in that direction, and that even as it was being positioned, a fireman already was climbing it.

Apparently, the man framed in the window could not see the ladder coming to his rescue. He kept peering behind him, and then he turned full face to the window. Swinging his right leg over the window ledge, he covered

his face with his arm as he prepared to jump. He teetered
off balance as he brought his second leg out of the window. Just before he fully cleared the window and dropped
into a free fall, the firefighter on the ladder reached out
and caught him in a bear hug. Somehow, the fireman
managed to attach a harness to the clinging boy as the
ladder was swiveled away from the burning building.

It was obvious that the fire was beating the efforts of
the firemen. No matter where their hoses were pointed,
new licks of flame could be seen sprouting through other
parts of the house and roof. Denney looked around for
Bill, but she still didn't see him. She started to go help
Ana and Marilyn, who, a few yards away on her right,
were leading dazed looking Phi Delts over to a grassy
circle in front of the Sorosis house where, without being
in the way of the rescue workers, one could see the dev-
astation that was taking place.

As she was about to join them, her attention was
drawn to the opening of the front door of the burning
building. A man, half pushing and half carrying another
person, stumbled through the doorway. Paramedics ran
to pull them to safety while firefighters sprayed more
water in their direction.

Relieving the man of his burden, the paramedics immediately began working on the apparently unconscious
victim. Waving off a different paramedic who approached
him, the first man's eyes never left the group working on
the still figure. It was only when there was a small chok-
ing sound, and the seemingly comatose person turned
his head and retched, that he looked back at the burning
fraternity house.

Flames now engulfed the doorway and probably the
path he had followed to escape the building. Watching

him, Denney shuddered. The possible outcome of his act of bravery haunted her.

Paramedics were readying the now conscious boy for placement in the ambulance. From his gurney, he apparently called out to his rescuer, who turned back towards him. He leaned over the gurney, as if listening, and then, as the paramedics raised the stretcher to put him into the ambulance, the two grasped hands for a moment. Only when the ambulance doors closed, did the soot-faced student begin walking towards the Sorosis lawn where most of the students were congregated. Looking at the boy favoring his left arm, Denney realized it was Bill.

She tried to run to him, but an officer doing crowd control stopped her. "Bill," she called around the officer, but he didn't hear her. As she argued with the policeman, she saw Willoughby break through the Washtenaw Avenue side of the crowd and reach Bill's side. For a moment, Bill recoiled from Willoughby, but then it became apparent that in true form, Willoughby had grabbed Bill's injured arm as he tried to guide him towards a car parked at the curb. In what appeared to almost be a comical sequence, Willoughby managed to hit the arm at least one more time as he helped Bill into the front seat of the car. Rather than getting in the car with Bill and the driver, Willoughby turned to face the Sorosis house as the car pulled away.

Seeing Denney, Professor Willoughby made his way over to her. "Where did Bill go?" she demanded.

Standing in front of her in his tweed jacket with suede patches on its sleeves, Willoughby looked more like he should be standing on the lawn at a hunting lodge rather than amidst fire debris. "To University Hospital. Mrs. Henderson is taking him to the emergency room to have a burn on his arm examined. Considering the stunt he pulled, he really is a very lucky guy." Willoughby was still talking to air as Denney ran back towards the sorority house wondering whose car she could borrow.

The lobby and dining room of the house were filled with partially dressed Phi Delts being ministered to by various members of Collegiate Sorosis. Sorority members, with the help of the Sorosis housemother, were handing out quilts, oversized sweaters, and other t-shirts and clothing the girls had scavenged for the fire refugees.

The person most in her element was Marilyn. Demonstrating a professional would-be nursing demeanor, she was carefully taking the pulse and temperature of a young man whom Denney recognized as Brian, the president of the Phi Delts. Watching the cheerful, but efficient manner in which Marilyn was handling the situation, Denney almost thought Marilyn had redeeming features. From the way Brian was looking at Marilyn as she held his wrist, it was obvious that he apparently thought so, too. Denney wondered if his temperature was rising.

Normally, Denney would have stopped to help, but she felt an urgent need to get to the emergency room. Spotting Ana guiding two Phi Delts towards the dining room, where a soup and sandwich lunch had been put on the buffet, Denney waved to catch her eye. She made her way through the lobby towards Ana and quickly explained that Bill was in the emergency room and that she needed to find a car to borrow. "I'll go with you," Ana said. "I can probably borrow our housemother's car again."

As Ana started for the dining room where their housemother was handing a denim shirt to a small man who looked like he had little to nothing under the quilt wrapped around him, Denney stopped her. "Ana, I just remembered Bill put his keys on my dresser. I don't think he picked them up when we ran out of my room. If my memory is right, we could just take his car." Moments later, Denney was back on the main floor, with her purse on her shoulder and Bill's keys in her hand. Together, they walked to Bill's Mustang.

# THIRTY-ONE

*Wednesday, December 8, 1971*

THE EMERGENCY ROOM was a zoo. Phi Delts, adding to the regular emergency patient load, were either in treatment rooms or in the waiting room. The feeling of general confusion was enhanced as friends and family members arrived seeking information about the various Phi Delts who has been brought in. Denney and Ana pushed through the people milling around in front of the receptionist's desk. Catching the receptionist's attention, Denney blurted out, "Bill Smythe, please." Ignoring others who argued that they had been there first, the receptionist checked the computer, and indicated that nobody with that name had been brought in. "But Professor Willoughby said they were bringing him here," Denney said confusedly, looking around the waiting room to see if Mrs. Henderson was there.

Before Denney could move, Ana leaned in front of her and said, "I think it would be under Willard Smythe, spelled S-M-Y-T-H-E." Denney was surprised that Ana, who she thought was barely acquainted with Bill, apparently knew his given name when she did not. Without even checking her computer, the receptionist pointed to a pair of metal doors, and indicated that Willard Smythe was being seen in Treatment Room 4. Thanking her, the two started towards the doors, but the receptionist brought them up short with an icy stare, as she admonished them, "You can't go back there if you're not related."

"No problem," Ana said sweetly, continuing to move towards the doors. "We're his sisters." Seeing the receptionist look from one to the other in disbelief, Ana smiled. "We have different mothers. Dad likes variety." Ana pulled her dumbfounded sister through the doors before the receptionist could say anything else.

They burst into Treatment Room 4, with Denney leading the way. Standing in front of them was Dr. Oliver. He was instructing Bill to "Keep this dry for a few days" as he finished taping a gauze pad on Bill's upper arm. Mrs. Henderson was nowhere to be seen. Seeing Denney and Ana, Bill smiled sheepishly. Jack Oliver also looked pleased to see them. "How's my most unusual patient and her friend?"

Ignoring Jack, Denney walked straight up to Bill and yelled, "You idiot! You could have been killed!"

"Don't you think, 'Hi Bill' or 'Are you all right?' would be a little more compassionate sounding than 'You idiot!'?" Bill asked.

Perhaps it was Dr. Oliver's laughter at this exchange or the contrast between Bill's suggestion and what she was thinking as she took in his bandaged arm and the whiteness of his teeth against his charcoal-stained face, but she felt another wave of anger. She forced herself to stay in control. "Are you all right?"

"Just fine," he said and grinned. But, looking him over, she could see that he was not fine. In addition to his bandaged arm, it was apparent the fire had burnt small holes in his shirt and pants. The tassel of his right loafer appeared to have been cleanly severed, yet the left loafer looked as if it had just come out of a box. Following her eyes, he shrugged and said, "I guess I kicked something with my shoe."

"And your arm?" she asked.

"Must have bumped something. The bandage makes it look worse than it is," he assured her. "It's a big nothing."

"Not such a big nothing," Dr. Oliver interjected. "You have a pretty deep burn, and we don't want it to get infected. Like I told you, don't get that arm wet for the next week. You'll need to change the dressing twice a day, putting on some of this antibiotic salve each time," he said, handing Bill a slim tube. "I want to see you again before next weekend."

"Yes, doctor," Bill replied with a mock salute.

"At ease, son," Jack Oliver told Bill, who could only have been, at most, four or five years his junior. "One more thing," he said as Bill looked up expectantly. "You were a pretty lucky guy today with that stunt you pulled and Moose is definitely a very alive guy today thanks to you, but watch yourself," Jack warned. "You keep doing things like this, and you could get hurt a lot worse."

"Come on, Jack," Bill said with obvious familiarity, "you would have done the same thing if you had been at the house today." At this, Denney and Ana exchanged confused looks. Noting their reaction, Bill explained. "Jack was an active pledge while he was an undergrad. He now is one of our alumni board members."

"Does everybody at Michigan have a connection to the Phi Delt house?" Denney asked incredulously.

"Only those that matter," Bill joked.

Disregarding this light-hearted banter, Jack again focused on Bill. "Bill," he said quietly. "You've got to take your responsibility seriously. Remember what Ferguson told you last night. A lot of people believe you're worth investing in, but you only have so many lives. You've got to be careful."

"Not at Moose's expense. I knew he still had to be in there and that nobody would remember where he landed this time. Moose kind of floats and drops wherever he passes out," Bill explained to the girls, almost apologetically.

"Moose?" Ana asked.

"His real name is Peter Franklin Foster, III," Jack said.

"Like the millionaires Peter Foster senior and junior who are associated with Foster Hall?" Denney inquired, as she made the connection between the name and a family that had made a fortune selling scrap iron for military purposes during World War II and then the Korean War. When the family had donated money for the Foster building a few years ago, there had been protests about it being blood money because of their little known involvement in munitions for the Vietnam War.

"That's right, but we call him Moose. He got that nickname back in kindergarten at the Normal Day School, when he was assigned to be a reindeer in a production of Rudolph the Red Nosed Reindeer. His housekeeper didn't know the difference between a moose and a reindeer so she got him a Bullwinkle costume. The other little children came prancing out as sweet reindeer with little tails or horns, followed by Bullwinkle the Moose. After a few weeks of being referred to as Bullwinkle the Moose, the kids shortened his nickname to Moose, and it stuck. He couldn't even get away from it at college as so many of us have gone all the way through school together."

"I didn't know you went to Normal Day." But then again, Denney thought, I didn't even know your real name. "What I don't understand is how you were the only one who knew where Moose was at the time of the fire?"

"It was an educated guess. Last night, we had a frat meeting. This is the one meeting a year that includes actives, advisors and board members. You know our actives, most of the guys feel the need to have liquid refreshment present no matter what kind of meeting we have. Moose likes his a little too much, but he can't hold it. He started drinking before the meeting ever began, and by the time it ended, he was pretty well gone. Our general practice is to leave him wherever he is to sleep it off, but if one of us is feeling generous, we rouse him and guide him to the sleeping porch or to his room. I was probably the last student to leave, and I left him there. This morning, when I saw the fire was on the floor near the meeting room, I immediately thought of Moose and knew I had to do something."

"You could have told the firemen instead of bursting in there yourself," Jack admonished. "You've got to think."

"I know. I'll try to do better," Bill said.

"It isn't funny. I give up on you," Jack laughed. "Tell you what," he said to Denney and Ana, "if you have a car, you can take this bozo home."

"No problem. We brought his car." Ana held up Bill's car keys. "We're good," she said anticipating Bill's surprised look. Denney just grinned when he looked at her.

Jack was leaving the room when they heard his name paged over the loudspeaker. He grabbed the phone on a nearby wall, punched in a four digit extension, and barked: "Oliver." He listened for a moment and then hung up the receiver. "Looks like they found another person in the fire. The paramedics are bringing him in now, but it doesn't look good." Jack began striding towards the ambulance entrance.

As Denney, Bill and Ana left the treatment room, they could see other members of the trauma team moving in the same direction that Jack had gone. In the meantime, a nurse began cleaning the room they had just vacated. The three were still standing just outside the treatment room door when the automatic glass emergency entrance doors burst open. Two paramedics rushed in pushing a gurney. The three watched as the trauma team began taking a history from the paramedics while working on the patient.

Pressing themselves against the wall, the three watched the synchronization of the team's actions as Dr. Oliver yelled quick orders. With so much going on, it was only a matter of seconds before the gurney passed. Even from the quick look they were able to get before the patient was whisked into room 4, there was no mistaking who it was: Dr. Ferguson.

# THIRTY-TWO

*Wednesday, December 8, 1971*

STUNNED BY WHAT they had just seen, Denney, Bill and Ana remained frozen in front of the closed door. From the sounds within Treatment Room 4, they knew that the trauma team was actively working on Dr. Ferguson. Hearing commotion to their left, they looked towards the ambulance entrance to see Kellie, Dr. Harris, and Professor Willoughby coming through the same door that the gurney had passed through just moments before.

"Ferguson?" asked a distraught looking Kellie.

"They're working on him, in there." Denney pointed.

Kellie immediately reached for the door pull, but Bill stopped her by catching her arm. "I think we'd all better wait out here," he suggested. "It's pretty crowded in there, and I think we'd just get in the way."

"Is he alive?" Kellie gasped out between sobs.

"I don't know," Bill answered, relinquishing his hold on Kellie's arm. Ana stepped forward to steady Kellie. "What happened to him?" he asked Professor Willoughby and Dr. Harris.

"He was still in the Phi Delt house," Dr. Harris replied. "Sean and I were on the lawn watching the Phi Delt insignia twist and burn when word went out that the firemen had found another person."

"I was waiting for Mrs. Henderson to come back from taking you," Professor Willoughby said. "Mrs. Henderson called me to meet her at the house this morning. We were going to finalize some of the Mudbowl details, but when she pulled up, the fire already was going. You came out just then and we thought it best she take you here. I was waiting for her to get back," Willoughby added again, as if he needed to explain why he had ended up on the lawn with Dr. Harris.

"She must have forgotten she was coming back to meet you because she called Aunt Maisie from here for me and then volunteered to go pick her up. Aunt Maisie wasn't going to be happy until she could see for herself that I'm okay. I'm surprised they're not here yet."

"I don't understand," Denney said.

"Remember, Mrs. Henderson has known Aunt Maisie for years and knows she doesn't drive. Aunt Maisie was so upset about the fire and the fact that I was hurt, that she wanted to come over here immediately. Rather than making her walk or take a cab, Mrs. Henderson kindly offered to go get her. She was pretty upset about the fire, too."

"She must have forgotten me after she saw the confusion down here," Professor Willoughby said. "I certainly hate that we're going to have to tell Brenda and Maisie about Ferguson being in the fire, too."

"He was in the building?" Bill asked.

"Yes. The firemen were working their way through the rooms to make sure that there were no more hot spots and that everybody had been accounted for. They found him in the meeting room." A look of anguish passed across Bill's face. It heightened when a downcast Dr. Oliver came out of Treatment Room 4. Not quite looking at their anxious faces, he said, "I'm sorry. He's gone."

Denney and Bill stared at Jack. Kellie began to cry uncontrollably on Ana's shoulder. Awkwardly, Dr. Har-

ris reached out to pat Kellie's hair. Professor Willoughby
stood alone, stunned. "Was it smoke inhalation?" Denney asked.

   "That may have contributed to his death, but I think
the bash somebody gave him on the back of his head
probably had more to do with it," Jack said. "We'll have
to do some testing to determine the actual cause of death,
but I'd bet foul play was involved."

# THIRTY-THREE

*Wednesday, December 8, 1971*

Sergeant Rutledge did not look amused. Standing in the Sorosis quiet lounge, he surveyed the faces of the Phi Delt and Sorosis coeds who had been assembled at his request. Denney peered around the room, trying to see things as he was seeing them. Most of the Phi Delts were as subdued as they had been when they learned of their advisor's death. The majority were now wearing more normal looking attire, but a few still had on outfits that the girls had pulled together for them.

Bill was one of these. He had planned to wait for Aunt Maisie before going to his apartment to change, but Sergeant Rutledge specifically requested that he go directly to the Sorosis house. Although Sergeant Rutledge had tried to assure him that he or one of his officers would advise her of what had happened to her ex-husband, Bill had been adamant that he needed to be there when she was told. Sensitive to the situation, Rutledge relented, permitting Ana, Denney, and Kellie to wait with him.

Denney had been surprised when Aunt Maisie and Mrs. Henderson arrived. She had expected to see a down-trodden middle-aged woman, but in reality, Maisie was a pleasing looking trim woman with short highlighted hair. Her well-chosen colorful clothing accentuated her youthful figure. It was Mrs. Henderson who actually looked worse today. Her skewed scarf, soot-smudged skirt, and smoke reddened blue eyes, gave her a far more disheveled appearance than Aunt Maisie. Denney guessed that Aunt Maisie was a person who put little stock in makeup or show when she dressed, but on whom, even as she aged, things just looked right. Her only concern, after assuring Bill that she had already called his mother, had been to check for herself that he really was fine. She had looked him over from head to tail, and satisfied herself that he would live before she really became conscious of the others waiting with him.

Sergeant Rutledge had given them the briefest of moments for introductions before he ushered Mrs. Henderson, Aunt Maisie, Bill, and Professor Willoughby into one of the other treatment rooms so that the women could have an element of privacy when they learned the bad news. Standing outside the door, Denney was sure she could hear crying.

After awhile, Bill came out of the room with Sergeant Rutledge, leaving the others inside. "I've suggested that Mr. Smythe go home with you since I understand you have his car," he said to Denney, Ana, and Kellie. "I've called ahead and asked your housemother to round up all the Phi Delts and Sorosie at your house for a meeting in about an hour," he said, consulting his watch. "I would appreciate it if you would be present, too."

"We'll try, but we should take Bill home, first," Ana responded, looking at Bill's bandaged arm with concern.

"He doesn't need any more meetings," Denney said, thinking that the silent Kellie did not need to be at a meeting with the police, either.

"No, I would like all of you there." Sergeant Rutledge's voice was more a command than a request.

Denney started to protest, but Bill stopped her. "It isn't a problem," he said. "Mrs. Henderson and Professor Willoughby are going to make sure Aunt Maisie gets home safely." The fact that Bill had given up so easily bothered Denney. Watching his discussion with Rutledge, she had felt that the events of the day were overwhelming his usual levelheadedness, blinding him to what Sergeant Rutledge was really doing.

From what she could see going on behind him while Bill and Rutledge talked, it appeared that Sergeant Rutledge was taking no chances this time in terms of isolating and questioning witnesses. An officer she didn't know had taken Dr. Harris into one of the treatment rooms, something she didn't feel a need to interrupt Bill or Rutledge to mention. Denney felt certain that Sergeant Rutledge also would have Aunt Maisie, Mrs. Henderson, and Professor Willoughby interviewed before he let them leave.

After Sergeant Rutledge explained the arrangements for the meeting at Sorosis, he let them go. Kellie rode in silence with them back to the sorority house and went directly to her room to have a few minutes alone before the meeting. Ana took Bill into the kitchen to wash up and to check to see if the pantry still had any extra clothing.

Left alone, Denney wandered around the Sorority house. Many of the boys were happily eating in the dining room. Bandages here and there indicated that their medical needs also had been met. The lobby had been cleaned up by shifting most of the things the Phi Delts had rescued to the downstairs study room. That room apparently had been converted into temporary quarters for the displaced Phi Delts to use dorm style for a few nights, until other arrangements could be made for them.

Denney felt overcome by a great sense of uselessness after seeing Marilyn in the dining room in the center of a group of Phi Delts. Whatever she had done, Marilyn now

had a devoted following, including an obviously smitten
Brian. For a moment, Denney felt a wave of self-pity,
and then she realized that she was just overtired. After
all, she thought, she had just gotten out of the hospital
herself, and today had been more than a little emotional.

Her mood lightened as she saw Bill and Ana returning.
His shirt had been replaced with a white serving jacket.
The absurdity of the starched white serving jacket contrasted against his burnt pants and shoes made Denney
laugh out loud.

"You don't like my tailored look," he observed, as
the three of them joined the group gathering in the quiet
lounge for the meeting with Sergeant Rutledge.

"The height of elegance," she replied, laughing anew.

Entering the room, Denney and Bill sat on the floor
near a group of the Phi Delts, while Ana waited by the
door for Kellie. Personally, Denney was not convinced
that Kellie would voluntarily reappear for Rutledge's parlor meeting, but as he began addressing the assembled
students, a very pale Kellie entered the room. She sat
down, Ana protectively flanking her. It was obvious that
she had been crying.

"I'm Sergeant Jim Rutledge. This is Officer Paul Topazi," he said pointing to a small dark-haired man standing beside him. Denney noted that the junior officer was
a good ten years younger than Sergeant Rutledge. More-
over, his shoulder insignia had fewer stripes on it. "We
know that today's fire, and especially the passing of Dr.
Ferguson, has been a real shock to you. We're sorry to
have to intrude on you at this time, but we owe it to Dr.
Ferguson." Despite a few sobs here and there, the majority of the students were now listening carefully to Sergeant Rutledge as he explained that Dr. Ferguson had not

died of smoke inhalation. At the mention of murder, he had the students' full attention.

"We understand that this is a sensitive time for many of you who knew Dr. Ferguson well, but we also are aware that with the burning of the Phi Delt house, most of you will only be under the Sorosis roof tonight, and then will be disbursing throughout campus in the next few days. Consequently, we feel we owe it to Dr. Ferguson to speak to as many of you as we can while you are together. Either Officer Topazi or I will talk with you. We appreciate your time and will make every effort not to detain you too long. Once we have finished speaking with you, you will be free to leave, but we would prefer you don't discuss this matter among yourselves."

Listening to Rutledge doing a poor imitation of Mayberry's Sheriff Taylor, Denney was put off by how he was working the crowd. From the rear of the room, Denney could hear soft sobbing. She knew without looking that it was coming from Kellie. A glance back towards her friends confirmed her suspicion, and the harsh anger she had felt at Rutledge the other night was rekindled. Without thinking, she found herself rising and facing him. "Sergeant Rutledge, there are a lot of people here who are sick over Dr. Ferguson's death. There also are many who are physically ill from the effects of the fire. These people need to be allowed to rest and have medical and spiritual attention rather than being exposed to police interrogation."

For a moment, there was silence in the room. Then, others picked up her refrain. "This man here is running a fever," one of the Phi Delts said, pointing at Bill. "I think I inhaled too much smoke to be interviewed today," another said coughing for emphasis. "Don't we have the right to have lawyers present?" asked a young woman.

The lines in Sergeant Rutledge's face became more hardened, and he lost the hokey small-town attitude he had been projecting as he responded: "This is not a formal interrogation. You do not have to participate nor do you have to have a lawyer present. You can if you want."

"Maybe we could do this tomorrow when people are feeling better?" Marilyn asked, as she smiled at Brian.

"Yes," Brian said, also now on his feet, "I'm the president of the Phi Delt house, and I can assure you that we are keeping up where each house member is. Sergeant Rutledge, even if somebody doesn't stay here after tonight, we'll know where to find him."

"Most of them will be here for a few nights," Sorosis' president piped up. "We're letting them sleep in our downstairs study room so everyone should be here in the morning. You probably could get more information from all of us after a good night's sleep," she suggested.

"Now, folks, it always is better for you to talk to us while things still are fresh in your memories," Officer Topazi said trying to soothe the room. "One never knows what little fact you might not even know you know that could make a difference in our solving Dr. Ferguson's murder in a timely manner. You have the right to have representation while we talk, but if you have nothing to hide, there shouldn't be a problem. Time is really of the essence in solving a brutal crime like this. Surely you understand."

It was obvious that except for a few pockets here and there, Officer Topazi's remarks had shifted the mood of the room back towards voluntarily being a good citizen and talking with the police immediately. Taking advantage of the momentum towards cooperation, Sergeant Rutledge reverted to a simple way of speaking as he urged all who were willing to talk to him to please raise their hands so that Officer Topazi and he could divide them up. "Those of you who don't feel up to talking today, please step into the living room for a moment so we can get your names. We'll formally arrange to speak with you in the next few days. Again, today is purely voluntary."

"But, if anyone would like representation, even if only for today, I'll be glad as Phi Delt counsel of record to make myself available for your interview," a voice said from the doorway. All eyes turned in the direction of the speaker. He was a good-looking, well-built man with pale golden hair, flecked with a gray which reflected light. His athletic stance, coupled with a pug nose that obviously once had been broken and not repaired gave Denney the feeling that he could be a true street fighter even though the cut of his clothing yelled tailor-made.

As impressive as the man was, the woman standing just behind him drew all attention away from him. Tall and stately, she commanded attention without asking for it. She was simply beautiful. Her hair was pulled back with an old-fashioned cloth hairband, and she wore no makeup to accentuate her washed-out blue eyes. Her dress was an off-the-rack A-line, but its simplicity highlighted how naturally stunning she was. An immediate whispered undercurrent spread through the room as people recognized her from her picture being on the society and business pages of both the Detroit and national newspapers.

Although Denney had known that Bill's father was a prominent Detroit lawyer, she had not made the connection that Willard Rocklin, one of the country's most well-known private philanthropists, was his mother. Now, looking from one to the other, there was no mistaking whose son he was.

The history of the Rocklin family's largess at the University was well-known because of its uniqueness. Rather than endowing buildings at the University of Michigan and other institutions of learning, the Rocklin Family Foundation created scholarships. The Rocklins also were generous in response to many other community and civic needs, but usually anonymously.

If Denney remembered the story correctly, the original patriarch, Willard Rocklin, was born to poor farmers. Times and the land being hard, he was forced to spend much of the school year helping his parents plant and harvest what little crops they could, but a spinster teacher recognized his brilliance and worked with him at night. She arranged for him to have an opportunity, as a charity case, to attend the University of Michigan.

He arrived on campus with ten dollars she had given him, enough to get a room and meals until he could find honest labor. He had tried to assure her he would work hard and repay her as soon as he could, but she had silenced him by telling him that she needed nothing more than for him to graduate, live modestly, and give back to others.

The first term at Michigan was difficult for Willard Rocklin, but his final grades were everything his now late mentor believed he could accomplish. Rocklin graduated with an engineering degree, and went to work for one of the major Detroit automakers. Much as he tried, he was unhappy being one of a group of engineers, so he resigned and opened a pipe manufacturing company. He carved out a specific niche for his product and after inventing a means for processing pipe cheaper and more efficiently than his competitors, he was able to buy most of them out. The need for his product escalated when America entered the war, and he took full advantage of it. Soon, he was one of the richest businessmen in America, but the general public did not know him because he had taken his teacher's advice to heart.

That probably would have been the end of the Rocklin story, but at fifty, he fell in love with a much younger woman. They had one son, Willard Rocklin, Jr., who continued to pursue his father's philosophy of earning money, and making generous donations anonymously. His only child, Willard Rocklin, III, formally created the Rocklin foundation, which his daughter now chaired.

It was obvious that today the Smythes had only one primary interest: their son. At the moment, Willard Rocklin was on campus only as a concerned mother, and Sergeant Rutledge had the intelligence to appreciate this fact. He immediately softened his approach, and let the students divide up as had been suggested. While he took the names of those who preferred to be interviewed in the morning, he sent those who didn't feel they needed counsel present to the dining room area with Officer Topazi. He waited patiently with the remaining students to allow Mr. Smythe and his wife to have some private time with their son. Then, with Bill's father present, he began his interviews.

Ana and Kellie quickly left the room, but Denney and Bill had agreed to be interviewed with Mr. Smythe present. For his own reasons, Sergeant Rutledge chose to save them until his last two interviews. At Bill's request, transmitted through his father, Sergeant Rutledge made a concession to the fact that Denney had just gotten out of the infirmary by permitting her to rest in her room until he was ready for her.

While Denney was upstairs, the Sorosis housemother, equally impressed as the others were with meeting Bill's mother, made the sitting room of her two-room apartment available to Mrs. Rocklin-Smythe and her son to rest. She even went so far as to bring them tea before making herself scarce in her back bedroom. There, she immediately called the Theta's housemother to brag that the Willard Rocklin, whose son she personally had tended to after the fire, had had tea in her quarters and had expressed her deepest appreciation and desire to do something for her and the members of Sorosis for taking in the Phi Delts.

By the time Denney was paged for her interview, Bill and his mother were gone. He had left word with his father that although he was going back to Detroit with them tonight, unless he heard otherwise, he still planned to take Denney to dinner and the Sinclair rally on Friday. As Mr. Smythe carefully delivered Bill's message, she felt he was examining her, evaluating his son's date choice. Now, she wished she had done more than run a brush through her hair. She felt nervous and clumsy, until Bill's father smiled at her as he guided her towards the interview room. He had the kind of smile and touch that is so inclusive, it makes one feel that there is no one else in the room. Denney had read about this kind of aura that certain people, like many successful politicians, possess, but she had never really felt it herself before. She felt quite confident going into the interview room that she knew nothing of any pertinence and that even if she did, Mr. Smythe would protect her interests.

# THIRTY-FOUR

*Friday, December 10, 1971*

IT TOOK DENNEY all day Thursday and most of Friday to make up the assignments she had missed between her stay in the infirmary and the aftermath of the fire. She got back to the sorority house with a couple of hours to spare before Bill picked her up for the Sinclair rally. With the time she had, Denney debated between taking a shower or a quick nap first. She chose the nap, but found herself unable to sleep because she kept going over the events of the past few days in her mind.

She finally decided to give up the idea of napping and let herself concentrate on the connections between the Phi Delt house and Michigan's English department. Obviously, not everybody in the English department had a direct relationship to the Phi Delt house, but there were certainly a lot of coincidental ties. Mulling this over, Denney felt that if she could trace the different connections, she might be a step closer to figuring out who had murdered Dr. Ferguson and Helen and who had attempted to kill her.

As she automatically linked Dr. Ferguson and Helen's deaths, it chilled her to think that there was someone out there who thought so little of the value of human life that he or she had killed at least two people. The thought that the killer might kill again, or had already done so, was

completely disconcerting. She reined in her imagina-
tion, deciding to focus on the facts she knew rather than
on speculation.

Checking the clock, she decided that she still had
plenty of time before she had to be ready for Bill. She
opted to make a list of the similarities and differences
between Helen and Dr. Ferguson's murders. She threw
off the covers and grabbed a pen, notebook, and a folder
to lean on from a stack on her desk. After making herself
comfortable again on her bed, she opened the notebook to
a clean page which she titled: VICTIMS. She put Helen
and Ferguson's names as separate subheadings and then
used free thought associations to brainstorm her comparison list. Satisfied that she had run out of things to put
on the lists, she leaned back to reread them:

Ferguson
Male
Professor
English department-salaried
Poetry Specialty
Administrative figurehead
Hired Dr. Harris
Hit over the head with ? and left in burning building

Helen
Female
Student
English department-hourly
Middle English Specialty (?)
Student/order taker/staff slave
Friend of Dr. Harris
Hit over the head with a Chaucer bookend

Denney couldn't see any obvious clues or solutions. She decided to make a matrix wheel of everybody's connections to both Dr. Ferguson and Helen. Hopefully, at some point, something would jump out at her.

She put Dr. Ferguson's name in a circle in the middle of a different page in her notebook. From his name, she drew individual lines on which she placed the name of each of the different English department faculty members. She drew a solid line coming from Willoughby to a circle that represented Helen. From the circle, she used a dotted line between Helen and Dr. Ferguson to show that she had technically worked in his department. She also added dotted lines to show the other informal relationships between various faculty members, students, and non-university people.

Next to the dotted lines, she wrote, in small print, any connections she could think of between the various names. She documented things like Helen and Harris' shared teatime; the way Helen, Henderson, and Harris tied their scarves; the associative links to the Phi Delt house that she was aware of; the teachers up for tenure; which teachers had published together like Ferguson and Godbolt; who were working on the same projects like Willoughby and Henderson; and the personal relationships that created a connection to Ferguson such as with Aunt Maisie, Kellie, Bill, and Bill's parents.

Denney was nowhere near finished with Ferguson's matrix, and had not even started on one for Helen, when it became clear that although diagramming the connections was going to be helpful for organizational purposes, she would have to devise a better pictorial system for her analysis. Even with the limited amount of information she had put on her diagram, the lines and words were all running together.

She decided that time-wise, she better hit the showers. So, leaving the folder and notebook on her unmade bed, Denney picked up her towel and toiletry basket. She was about to go down the hall to take her shower, when she heard Marilyn's voice on her floor. As Denney waited just inside her bedroom door to let Marilyn clear the landing, Denney heard snatches of what sounded like a heated discussion about tomorrow's Mudbowl. Apparently, Marilyn still was complaining about Sorosis not being included. Denney felt a moment of anger that after everything that had happened, something as trivial as the Mudbowl could be considered so important.

Then, thinking about it, Denney realized that to the majority of students, Helen and Ferguson were names in news stories—to be acknowledged for a moment and then forgotten. Considering that to many of the students, the Mudbowl was the most important activity of the coming weekend, Denney felt a little badly that she had not designed a prank to avenge Sorosis' honor; but, she assured herself, people understood that she had been sick and then distracted by the fire and murders.

Once she was positive that the fire door had swung shut behind Marilyn, Denney left the safety of her room. The hot water striking her back felt good as she sang snatches of songs. Turning off the water and reaching for her towel, she thought about the irony that she could reel off pages of text verbatim, but could never remember song lyrics or joke punch lines. Her towel wrapped around her hair, Denney walked back to her bedroom to finish dressing.

Kellie was standing next to Denney's bed reading the notebook that Denney had been using for her detective work.

"What do you think you're doing?" Denney asked,

snatching at the notebook in Kellie's hand as she dropped her towel and toiletry basket on the floor.

"What do you think you're doing?" Kellie countered, refusing to relinquish the book. "This is my notebook."

"Excuse me? Your notebook?"

"Yes, my notebook," Kellie said, turning the notebook's bright green cover so Denney could see her name on it. "I must have left it here with my other books and folders." Seeing the confusion on Denney's face, she explained, "I've been looking for my science book all week, and during class, I remembered that I left some of my books in your room the night we went to the poetry party. You weren't here when I stopped by to get the books, but then I heard you singing in the shower so I didn't think you would mind my coming in to get my things."

"No more than when you help yourself to my clothes," Denney said, looking at the gray suit still sitting on her chair.

"I've offered to take that suit to the cleaners for you. Here let me have it," Kellie said, holding out her hand for the suit.

"Don't worry about it. Where are your books?"

"Right here." Kellie pointed to a short stack of books and folders on the corner of Denney's desk. "See, there's my science book. I was about to take my things and leave when I spotted my notebook on your floor."

"I left it on my bed."

"Well, I found it on the floor and I couldn't help seeing your notes. You walked in just as I realized what I was looking at. Honest, I wasn't snooping. It's not my fault you used my notebook. Here, take your pages back." She ripped out Denney's two pages and offered them to her. Denney took them without comment.

Looking uncomfortable, Kellie tried again. "Please,

Denney, this isn't something to be mad at me about. You
used my notebook and well, I wouldn't have kept reading your notes, it's just," she hesitated for a moment, before continuing, "it's just that I want to know who killed
Ferguson even more than you do." The sharp edge in her
voice caught Denney's attention.

"Do you have an idea who did it?" Denney asked.

"No, I just want to make sure that nobody I love did,"
she said simply. "Tommy met with Ferguson the day of
the fire."

"You never said anything about your brother meeting
with Ferguson."

"I didn't know until last night. He called and we were
talking about my tuition situation now that Ferguson is
gone. In the midst of our conversation, he casually mentioned that he had seen Ferguson the day he died to discuss how he treated me the night of the poetry party."

"You told Tommy about that night?" Denney asked
incredulously. "What did you want him to do, beat Ferguson up?"

"I don't know what I wanted. Things have been so
crazy…." Her voice trailing off, Kellie began to walk
to the window, but then she turned back to face Denney. Staring straight at her, she said, "The reason I was
in Ferguson's office the night of the poetry party is that
Tommy and Ferguson made a deal that required Ferguson to find makeshift work for me so that I can make
ends meet through the end of this term."

"What kind of deal?"

"Tommy wrote a book of poems, but in exchange for
Dr. Ferguson helping me, Tommy agreed to let Ferguson
take credit for some of the poems."

"But that's not right."

"That's how Ferguson works, I mean…worked. Who

do you think wrote the book he just published with Mr.
Godbolt? Godbolt did the work, but Dr. Ferguson was
listed as the primary author. I don't know what Godbolt
got out of the arrangement, but in Tommy's case, Dr.
Ferguson immediately called me to his office for a typing assignment."

"But you barely type."

"I know, but I can get by. I've typed other things for
him this year. Denney, Tommy sold his soul for me. I
thought I had no choice. So, I went. Dr. Ferguson gave
me a folder with the draft of his tenure recommendation
in it to type."

"Kellie, why would Dr. Ferguson give you the draft to
type? Ferguson is making these monumental decisions
affecting other people's lives, the two of you are anything but bosom buddies, and you expect me to believe
you ended up typing the recommendation? I don't think
so," Denney said sarcastically.

"You don't have to believe me, but the fact is that Dr.
Ferguson never learned to type. He either dictated or
wrote things out in longhand. Normally, the department
secretary typed his things for him, but when it was something he didn't want to get around, he would get a friend
or student assistant to type it in confidence outside of
the office. During the time we were together, I typed a
number of things for him. I'm sure Mrs. Henderson and
many of his other former students did, too."

"Do you know who he was going to recommend for
tenure?"

"No, I don't. I never read the recommendations because I was in such a hurry to get back here and meet
you. Then, in the confusion of Helen's death, Ferguson
turning on me again, your reaction, and the fire, I absolutely forgot I had left my books and things in here. Like

I said, I've been looking for my science book all week, but I completely forgot about leaving everything in your room until this morning."

"So, what prompted your memory?"

"Talking to Tommy last night. I had spoken to him after Helen's funeral about what happened before the poetry party and how the evening deteriorated. I begged him not to feel obligated to Dr. Ferguson. I told him I doubted Ferguson would ever really help either of us and might even be vindictive. Apparently, Tommy got so upset that, as my protective big brother, he came to Ann Arbor to pay Ferguson a personal visit. Denney, he saw him at the Phi Delt house the day of the fire."

"That doesn't prove anything," Denney noted.

"I know it doesn't prove anything, but Tommy has a temper. He intimated that he and Ferguson got into it physically. Denney, the police said Dr. Ferguson was hit in the head. If Tommy landed a good punch, he might have given him a concussion or something that caused Ferguson to pass out and not be able to escape. Tommy says Ferguson was fine when he left, but Denney, I'm petrified my brother might have killed Ferguson," Kellie confessed.

"Let's not jump to conclusions. At the hospital, Jack said Ferguson was bashed on the back of his head. If Tommy and he were fighting, Tommy would have hit him from the front. We just don't have enough information, but for the moment, Kellie, let it be. Ferguson hurt you enough, don't let him make you do something stupid," Denney urged. "It's easy to jump to conclusions. Look at me, I thought you were snooping through my things."

"Technically, except for the notebook being mine, I

guess I was prying," Kellie said sheepishly. "I'm sorry," she said, picking her things up from the desk.

Glancing beyond Denney, she pointed at the gray suit still lying on the chair. "Come on, let me take that suit to the cleaners today."

"To have another excuse to visit when I'm not here. No way," Denney said seriously, grabbing the suit. "Boy, does this reek. How much perfume did you spill on it?" she asked, sniffing at the suit.

"Quite a bit."

"Kellie, what scent is this? It smells familiar."

"I'm sure it does. That's the perfume Dr. Ferguson gave me and every woman in the English department. The irony is, as different as we all are, most of us liked it because it wore so well on all of us."

"That explains why in the hospital, I thought you were there, but I opened my eyes and it was Dr. Harris. She must have been wearing the same scent."

"Probably," Kellie agreed. "Everybody got it. One thing about Dr. Ferguson, he may have bought his holiday gifts in bulk, but he always had good taste." Kellie reached for the suit, but Denney refused to let her take it. Waving her off, Denney haphazardly threw the suit back onto the chair. Rather than trying again, Kellie acquiesced, saying: "All right. I won't take the suit, and I am sorry I read your notes." Raising her hand like a Girl Scout, she swore, "On my honor, I promise to keep my nose out of your things, and your clothes off my back."

Visualizing Kellie ringing doorbells and selling cookies as a Girl Scout, Denney began to laugh. "Hey," Denney said. "Don't make fun of that promise. I took my Girl Scouting days very seriously."

"I'm sure you did," Kellie teased, and then realized that Denney was telling the truth. Changing the sub-

ject, Kellie noted that besides picking up her things, she
had dropped in for another purpose. "The other reason
I came down is that Ana and I have some special plans
for tonight. We were hoping that since you feel better,
you would join us."

"I won't be around. I'm going to that Sinclair rally
with Bill."

"Well, we're not going out until quite late," she said,
without elaboration. "If you get back and want to go with
us, just let one of us know."

Denney didn't comment; her mind was racing. "Kellie,
if you've got the tenure recommendation, maybe there is
something there that would help us figure out who killed
Dr. Ferguson. Let's see it."

"I didn't think of that," Kellie said, putting her stack
back on the desk. She began rifling through the pile. "It
isn't here. The recommendation isn't here!" She immediately started looking around Denney's desk and the
floor behind it. As she moved books, papers, and folders, Denney stood still watching, a skeptical expression
spreading across her face.

"You don't believe me, do you?" Kellie asked.

"I don't know what to believe. You've told me so many
things," she said. "Better get your stuff because Bill will
be here any minute." Ignoring Kellie, Denney put on a
clean blouse and pair of jeans. She then gathered up her
own books and notebooks and placed them on the side
of the desk furthest from Kellie's things. Pointedly, she
stuck her notes about Dr. Ferguson and Helen into one of
her own notebooks. "Don't count on me for tonight. If I
should get back early and change my mind, I'll tell Ana."

Kellie did not respond.

With Kellie in front, they walked out of Denney's

room together, leaving the suit behind. Hesitating for a moment, Denney reached back and firmly closed the door to her room.

# THIRTY-FIVE

*Friday, December 10, 1971*

LOU'S WAS EXACTLY the hole-in-the wall dive that Bill had described when he had first asked her to go to the Sinclair rally. Crammed into a booth in the back corner, Denney had to agree that Bill also was right about the quality of the food. Since Bill had picked her up at the sorority house, the two had carefully kept their conversation centered on the restaurant, its food, and its proprietress.

He told her that the name of the restaurant was the nickname of its owner, Betty Lou. In naming her Betty Lou, her mother had envisioned pigtails and sweetness rather than heavily pancaked makeup and bleached hair. By her build and demeanor, Lou, as she preferred to be known, was a cross between a drill sergeant and a television missionary. Students, according to Bill, flocked to Lou's as much for doses of her practical no-nonsense advice as for her good Southern cooking.

When Denney and Bill entered the restaurant, it was immediately obvious who Lou was. As she ushered them to the rear booth, Denney could feel Lou's charcoal lined eyes evaluating her, and taking in the bandage on Bill's arm. "Heard you were quite a hero," Lou said.

"Not really. I think somebody has been exaggerating. It makes a good story, but don't put much stock in it."

"Well, Moose seems to think you walk on water," she said with praise in her eyes.

"That's what I mean. He wasn't awake so how could he know?" Bill joked. "Now tell me," he said, changing the subject, "do you have any of your special cheesecake tonight? Lou makes the best cream cheese cheesecake you ever tasted," he assured Denney as Lou hastened away to put two pieces aside for their dessert.

Denney still was contemplating her menu when Lou returned to take their orders. Although Bill ordered the house burger with onion rings, Denney decided that she needed comfort food. She placed an order for Lou's Special Recipe Southern Fried Chicken. Her order was met with a big grin from Lou. As Lou moved to another table, Bill leaned over and laughingly said, "You've just made a friend. Lou judges a person on whether they're an eater or not."

"So, being a bulk eater is in my favor?"

"Most definitely. She'll want me to marry you by next week."

"I think we should wait a little longer than that. After all," Denney said seriously, "marriage has to be built on trust. Why didn't you tell me about your Rocklin connection when I asked you about your picture in the annual the other day? Didn't you trust me?"

"It wasn't a matter of trust. It was a matter of being a Rocklin. Look at the discussion we're having right now. If I wasn't a Rocklin, we wouldn't be having this discussion."

"But you are a Rocklin. You can't hide from that. You're also a Smythe."

"True, but Denney, since I was a kid, people have been trying to get something from the Rocklins or me by trying to be my friend. I learned early on to keep that side of myself hidden in public," he said bitterly. Denney remain silent, hoping he would continue.

"When I was six, two important things happened. My dad's law practice gained national exposure from a big case that he defended, and just around the same time, my grandfather was killed in a plane crash. My mother was my grandfather's only child. Although she had been involved in the family foundation, my grandfather and she had envisioned she would learn the business in good time. When he died, there were people in the organization who wanted to step into his shoes, but my grandmother, Mary Rocklin, insisted that my mother assume control. She voted her shares and called in favors to block the opposition vote and insure my mother was named chair. I'm not sure my mother wanted to be in charge of the foundation, but my grandmother was right, she needed to be. She has the vision, skill, and work ethic necessary to increase its wealth and its philanthropic accomplishments."

"That must have been a hard time for you."

"Not really. But it could have been. That's the story I'm trying to tell you. You see, I'm the only child my parents were able to have. When they first married, before they ever had me, they promised each other that no matter what happened in their careers, they always would make time for each other and any children they had. Well, things were so crazy the year my grandfather died between my father's career and the unexpected meetings and things my mother had to attend, that they decided they should hire a nanny for me.

"They began the interview process by screening different agency candidates. One young woman was particularly attractive to them, but they couldn't quite bring themselves to make her an offer on the spot. Instead, they told her that they would have to check her references. They never checked her references because they sat up that night talking. They decided that to hire her would defeat their promise to each other so they came up with ways to raise me through inclusion in their business demands rather than shunting me off to the side with a nanny."

"That must have been a pretty big decision for them to make."

"Not to mention some of the sacrifices they each had to make to make it work," Bill said, "but I think we're a stronger family for it. The irony is that another family, the Fosters, hired the woman my parents almost hired."

"Your parents gave her to Moose's family?"

"No, she answered an ad that Moose's family placed for a nanny for Moose and his younger sister, Emily. The Fosters never checked her references before they hired her. The following weekend all of us were invited to a birthday party in West Bloomfield Hills for the child of one of the car executives. It was a free for all, with pony rides, balloons, clowns, and you name it. My parents took me, but Moose's parents sent Emily and him with the nanny. The party ended abruptly when somebody noticed Emily floating facedown in the family's pool. It turned out that the nanny was actually a reporter who had figured that she could get a scoop getting into people's homes by being a nanny to the rich and famous. When she got into the auto executive's home, she told six-year-old Moose to watch his three-year-old sister while she took off to explore the house. She swore she was only gone a few minutes, but whether it was a few minutes or whatever, she changed the lives of that family forever."

"Poor Moose."

"I was only six, but I remember everything from that day, especially what my parents said when they thought I was asleep. They realized that she could have been my nanny and that made them vow they must never lose

sight of our family life, and they didn't. I promised myself, probably taking things a little out of context, that I
would never let anybody get close to me because I was
a Rocklin. I decided I would follow the tradition of my
grandfather and great-grandfather."

"Pardon?"

"My great-great-grandfather, Willard Rocklin, Sr., believed in giving without publicity. He also decided that
for safety reasons, he would keep his family and himself out of the media. In keeping with his father's philosophy, Rock, Jr., refused to have his picture printed
in Michigan's student yearbook. He religiously avoided
personal publicity."

"A tradition that continues with you today?"

"I hope so," Bill admitted sheepishly. "Even my
mother doesn't have her picture in any of the yearbooks.
It was only when my dad made it big as a litigator that she
was forced, for his sake, to permit her likeness to appear
in pictures with him. The deal she made with him, and
much of the Detroit media after the nanny incident, was
that she would pose for pictures related to him and some
of her charities so long as nobody photographed me."

"But she's in the paper regularly," Denney observed.

"True, but if you look carefully, the only current pictures they run are from things she is socially at with my
dad. An old file photo is used anytime they run a story
about the foundation or her riches. I admit it is a weird
compromise, but it has worked for her and for us as a
family. I hope you believe me. I didn't lie to you because
I didn't trust you."

"No, you just omitted basic facts."

"Wait a minute, I distinctly remember telling you the
other night when we were discussing the freshmen book
that there were a lot of things I didn't know about you and

that you didn't know about me. I said I would be willing to share and learn. Remember?"

"Touché," Denney said with a laugh of relief. "I have one more question though."

"Shoot, or maybe I shouldn't say that the way things have been going lately," he said somewhat seriously.

"Bill, how did you know Moose was still in the meeting room?"

"Well, like I told you before, Ferguson had called the annual special meeting the night before the fire."

"What do you mean annual special meeting?" she asked.

"Once a year, the Phi Delts hold a meeting where everybody has to come because we vote on a lot of important things. Obviously, our main advisor, Dr. Ferguson, is there as well as other faculty, board, and non-active members who have a Phi Delt connection to what we vote on. For example, Mrs. Henderson was there as the sweetheart advisor because we were picking our fraternity sweetheart. Jack Oliver and some of the other alums were there for the main reason that the meeting is held."

"Which is what? You're losing me here. I know the sweetheart is the girl that the fraternity designates as the one they will serenade and usually make their Mudbowl queen, but that wouldn't need a special meeting."

"Look, I really can't talk about it. It's a secret," he said uncomfortably, looking around to make sure nobody was listening to their conversation. Watching him squirm, it dawned on Denney that the Phi Delts were part of the Greek system with its secret rites that included picking members to be part of university secret societies. She had heard about different societies like Skull and Bones at Yale, but she now realized there must be a similar one at Michigan.

Denney had never given much thought to how individuals were selected for these secret groups, but she knew that the people chosen were effectively in a secret power club both for campus and future life. Positive that was what he was alluding to, she was about to ask him if he was the anointed Phi Delt for this year, but thought better of pressing for further details if she wanted to have a nice evening. She steered Bill back to discussing Moose being in the meeting room.

"Well, Moose wasn't too into the meeting. He just kept drinking, and he passed out on the couch about the time the meeting broke up. There were still a few of us in the room talking to Dr. Ferguson, and then pretty much everybody left except for Ferguson, Moose and me. I was going to rouse Moose and help him back to his room, but I hate to admit it, I had had a few more than I should have had, too. Dr. Ferguson and I started talking and one topic led to another and well, let's just say things got out of hand. We cleared the air about a lot of things, but I stomped out of there leaving Dr. Ferguson to deal with Moose."

"You went home?"

"No, it was so late or early, depending on how you want to look at it, and I had promised to pick up your friends for breakfast, so I just crashed for a few hours on the fraternity's sleep porch. It was empty so I just grabbed a bunk." Denney had not seen a fraternity sleep porch, but she knew they were barracks-like sleeping rooms where guys slept outside of their designated rooms. The porches actually dated back to when more students were assigned a bedroom than there were beds in the room. In those days, the pledges were given a dresser in the bedroom, but were forced to sleep on the porch. Today, the porches were used mainly for drop-ins like Bill had been or for guys whose rooms were otherwise occupied.

"When I got up, I cleaned up a bit and then picked up Ana and Kellie. Until you and I were on the lawn and we saw that stereo thrown from the third floor, I hadn't given Moose another thought. But, at that moment, I realized he probably was still sleeping it off and that nobody would have thought to check for him in the meeting room. Everyone would have thought somebody else took him back to his own room or the sleeping porch—areas that people had already checked. When I didn't see him on the lawn, I just knew he still had to be in the house. It was my fault he got left in the meeting room." Bill squeezed a package of sugar. "I couldn't leave him there."

"You were right," Denney said, shuddering to think what Moose's fate might have been. "I don't want to get you upset, but if you found Moose in there, how did you miss Dr. Ferguson?"

"I don't know, Denney. I keep asking myself the same question. No matter how many times I visualize it, I remember it the same way. Moose was on the couch. I walked across the room to get him, and I carried him out the way I came in. I swear I never saw Dr. Ferguson in the main part of the room. If I had, I would have tried to get them both out," he said solemnly.

"I know you would have," she said, reaching to hold his hand. Just then, Lou appeared with their food. Noting them pull apart from the hand-holding to make room on the table for their meals, Lou gave them a big smile. As she walked away, both Bill and Denney tried to suppress giggles.

"You're right," Denney said, trying to swallow her laugh. "She is going to have us married off by next week."

# THIRTY-SIX

*Friday, December 10, 1971*

Leaving Lou's, Bill and Denney walked slowly towards Crisler Arena. They talked about the new campus buildings as they passed them, and how the weather would probably stay nice as both had brought umbrellas in response to the local weathercast. It was as if they had made an unspoken pact to enjoy the evening.

As they got closer to the arena, Denney wondered if the rally would draw a good crowd, as there had been so much advertising on the radio for it. "Probably," Bill replied. "The radio guys have been encouraging people to go all week. They want their listeners to show support for the $5 law." The $5 law which treated being caught with marijuana as a misdemeanor punishable by a $5 fine had created quite a controversy. Most students liked it, but the townies were against it. The print media in Ann Arbor had come out against the ordinance arguing that its implementation was a tragedy for Ann Arbor that would result in the community going to the derelicts and becoming an unsafe place to raise children. "I figure there will be picketers outside, but I don't know what kind of turnout you'll get for the actual concert."

"They really haven't named a lot of the acts," Denney observed. "Except for Commander Cody and His Lost Planet Airmen, I can't really think of any others."

"That's because most of the ads have named Commander Cody and His Lost Planet Airmen, but have only talked in terms of a star-studded lineup. Nobody knows quite who is going to appear, but for a couple of hours, it should be enjoyable entertainment."

"I'm sure it will be. I'm glad you asked me."

"Guess we're not the only ones who thought this concert would be worth attending," Bill said letting out a low whistle as he surveyed the line of people wound halfway around Crisler Arena. Checking his tickets, Bill realized that the Sinclair rally was open seating so they would have to get in line, too.

They had been waiting about ten minutes, enjoying the antics of a group of students in front of them who were clowning around, when Denney heard her name being called. At first, she couldn't locate where the voice was coming from, but then she saw Ana and Jack Oliver, still wearing his white jacket, crossing the street. "There you are, sis," Jack called. Approaching them, he gave her a big hug for the benefit of the people behind her. "We've been looking all over for you two. Ana was afraid we would miss linking up because I was so late picking her up. The emergency room was packed and then we had a really serious case come in," he said loudly enough to make sure the people standing around Denney and Bill heard every detail as he adroitly steered Ana and himself into a position to break the line.

"You have a lot of…" Denney began as Jack engaged the people on either side of Bill and her in conversation. Seeing Denney's indignation at this turn of events, as well as Bill's oblivion to Denney's irritation at Jack's behavior, Ana burst out laughing. Denney was about to tell her off, too, when the humor of the situation and the smooth manner in which Jack had been able to manipu-

late everybody to include Ana and him into the line made
her start laughing, too.

The line finally moved forward as word spread that the
main doors were now open. Once inside, the four tried to
find seats in the lower level, but it was quickly apparent
that they would have to sit higher up. Together, the four
surged forward with the crowd climbing into the less de-
sirable upper regions of the arena. Just shy of nosebleed
land, they grabbed the first four seats they could find.

From their vantage point, they could barely see a small
platform stage in the center of the arena floor, but they
could clearly see two giant screens that had been erected
on either side of the stage. Both screens simultaneously
were projecting the same image of the stage. The view
on the screens now was of the equipment or occasionally of a tech person checking to make sure a microphone
was working.

Denney felt a sense of exhilaration that she wasn't
sure if she should attribute to the height of the seats or
the excitement that was being generated by having so
many people in Crisler Arena. People literally were running up and down the aisles waving at friends, stopping
the food vendors, and just genuinely having a good time
as they got settled. The mood was being enhanced by
music being piped over a loudspeaker.

Suddenly, the lights went out. For a moment, Denney
was frightened, and then an announcer's voice came over
the P.A. system welcoming everyone to the John Sinclair rally. In the dark, the voice began to tell the story
of Sinclair and his alleged unjust imprisonment and concluded by saying that although he could not physically
be present tonight, he was with the crowd through a
telephone hookup. As if on cue, lights began to flicker
in the audience.

"What are they doing?" Ana asked.

"They're either all lighting up at the same time, or they're showing their solidarity with Sinclair," Jack replied.

"From the sweet smell, I would say it is a little of both," Bill observed.

"You mean...." Denney began.

"Yup, Mr. Hodges and his buddies are all around you," Bill declared. As Denney started to look around, Bill quickly explained that he only meant that figuratively. While Jack and Bill found this to be grounds to share a chuckle at her expense, Denney felt embarrassed and slightly annoyed. Just then, the lights went up, and she decided that rather than get huffy, she would enjoy the show and her friends' company.

The first few acts were not groups that any of them recognized, but they were good. About an hour into the show, Commander Cody and His Lost Planet Airmen were introduced. As they played their set, with references to Sinclair and freedom, Denney, Bill, Jack and Ana took it all in by alternating watching the big screens and just watching the crowd in general. By the time the group was winding down, the audience was fully revved up. The lead singer then took the microphone and motioned for everyone to be quiet. It took awhile, but eventually he could be heard above the crowd noise. He explained that while his group was appreciative of being headlined, there were many others who felt as they did for what this rally stood for. Consequently, with their indulgence, some of his friends would now like to perform, too, beginning with Stevie Wonder. The crowd went wild—screams and stomping of feet showed their approval.

Moments later, Stevie Wonder was sitting center stage behind a keyboard or at least that is how it looked on the big screens. Denney had never been too fond of Stevie Wonder, but as he played, for the entire next hour, she sat riveted. He was a master showman, and his love of music came through even on the flat screen. As he finally reached the end of his set, Denney turned to Bill to tell him how much she had enjoyed the concert, but before she could say anything, she realized that Stevie Wonder was introducing another act.

Hours later, the acts were still coming on stage. What had begun as a two hour concert was now approaching its seventh hour as midnight had long come and gone. Each time a group finished, a polished voice came over the P.A. system to announce another performer or group. By now, the audience was truly mellow. A little earlier, Jack had attributed the calmness and happiness everybody seemed to be feeling to being contact high, but Denney wasn't so sure. She knew that no matter how tired she was getting, she was enjoying every moment of the concert.

As the group that was on left the stage, there was silence. Thinking the concert had finally ended, Ana bent to pick up her purse from near her feet. Before she could sit upright again, the lights dimmed and a hush came over the lower floor. Then, the voice announced: "John Lennon and Yoko Ono introducing a new song that John has just recorded: 'Imagine.'" Denney and her friends sat transfixed as John and Yoko began to sing of peace, brotherhood, and people living as one. After they finished the song, they turned to the cheering audience with a smile and then the lights went out. When the lights came up a few moments later, John Lennon and Yoko Ono were gone and the rally was over.

The last moments of the rally left everyone in such a peaceful mood that the crowd was actually congenial as it worked its way out of the building. The unity of the moment was reflected even in a tacit truce between Denney and Jack as the two found themselves walking in step together after Ana and Bill had been pushed slightly ahead by the exiting people. "They look like they're really getting along," Jack observed, as Bill took Ana's arm to steady her.

"Like us?" Denney joked.

"Maybe," Jack replied. "We did get off to a pretty bad start, didn't we?"

"We did. You certainly were infuriating."

"I could say the same about you, but I won't," he teased. "Tell me, where are you from?"

"Jackson, Michigan," she replied. "And you?"

"Traverse City." Holding up his right hand to depict the mitten shaped state, he pointed to a spot just to the side of his pinky. "It's up here."

"I know. I've been up there with my family for the Interlochen Arts Festival."

"Then you've been near where I grew up. My stepfather used to teach at the Interlochen Arts Academy."

"Did you go to high school there?"

"Yes, but I excelled in math and science rather than the creative arts. What made you pick Michigan?"

"Two reasons. First, my parents only can afford in-state tuition. I have a kid brother who will be starting college next year," she explained. "And, more importantly, at the time, my high school journalism teacher thought Michigan's journalism program would be a better match for me than the one at Michigan State."

"Why? Michigan State is known for having a great journalism school."

"That and the fact that I loved its campus is why I originally planned to go there, but she convinced me that I would do better with a less rigid program. I guess she was ahead of me in figuring out that journalism would only be one of the many majors I would end up exploring." .

Jack put his arm around Denney for a moment to keep her on the curb as the crowd jostled them. "So, what are you majoring in now?"

"English and history and, that's only because the majority of hours I've earned are concentrated in those two areas." Denney felt that it was better not to confess to Jack that one time going through the registration lines had been enough for her. Rather than waiting in line in future terms, she had signed her registration sheets with the names of different cartoon characters and then slipped in through the exit to deposit her forms in the checkout box. Consequently, she had tended to take classes that interested her or that she thought related to her major of the term rather than what would probably have been recommended. It was only this year, when she started thinking about whether she had the proper credits for graduation that she had finally taken her schedule to an academic advisor to review and sign off on.

After looking at her earned credits, the advisor had pointed out that she could have a double major if she went back and picked up History 102. He couldn't understand how she had been allowed to take so many upper level history courses when she never had taken the prerequisite 102 course. Denney didn't have the heart to tell him that she had skipped it because 101 was so boring.

"And after you graduate?"

"I don't know yet. I'm torn between going to New York to try to get a job in publishing or just going on to law school. How about you? Did you always want to be a doctor?"

"Ever since I was nine. I can't tell you why though. We don't have any other doctors in the family and nobody I knew ever had a major medical crisis. It was just one of those things that when someone asked me what I want to be when I grew up, I answered 'a doctor.' I've been answering that question the same way so long that I had to go through with it."

"Happily so, for me." Under a streetlight, she could see him smile as he reached for her hand. Together, they made their way forward with the others exiting the concert.

As the crowd began to thin out, Jack spotted Bill and Ana waiting for them on the opposite corner. Letting go of Denney's hand, he waved to catch their attention. After the light changed, Denney and Jack crossed and joined Bill and Ana to walk back to Sorosis. With "good nights" and "good mornings," Denney and Ana left the boys at the steps of the sorority house. Inside, they went straight to their rooms. Deciding that a shower could wait a few hours, Denney left her clothing strewn on the floor as she grabbed a long t-shirt and went right to bed. With the words of "Imagine" running through her head, Denney found herself drifting into sleep within moments of her head resting on her pillow.

# THIRTY-SEVEN

*Saturday, December 11, 1971*

MUDBOWL SATURDAY CAME earlier for Denney than she had intended. Having forgotten to draw her curtains when she went to bed after the rally, she was awakened by sunlight coming into her room. Rising early was so contrary to her normal body rhythms that it usually produced an immediate level of irritation, but today, her sense of calm from the night before carried over.

Fully awake at 6:00 a.m., according to the numbers on her bedside clock radio, she opted to have an early breakfast. She picked up the jeans she had worn the night before from the stack of clothing she had left on the floor. Seeing no obvious stains on them, she put them on and shoved the ends of her sleep shirt into the waistband. She slipped her bare feet into her sneakers and nimbly sidestepped the clothing and other school things that she had thrown from her bed onto the floor last night.

The kitchen was deserted. Somebody had stuck makeshift notes on the freezer and refrigerator doors that read: "Hungry? Eat Out. It's Mudbowl Day!" Denney actually was glad that the normal breakfast bustle had been dispensed with so none of her sorority sisters could confront her about the Mudbowl slight. Considering the ideas that Kellie, Ana, and she had brainstormed had had real possibilities, it really was a shame that she had been unable to get it together enough to avenge Sorosis' honor.

Oh well, that was something she couldn't control, but she could make sure she got something to eat. Denney decided to treat herself to breakfast at The Jugg. On the way there, she deliberately crossed Washtenaw so she could walk on the side of the street nearest to the Mud-bowl. From the soppy condition of the ditch, the hoses had been running all night. There actually was water standing in the basin. At the moment though, nobody was in the bowl, nor was anyone particularly watching it. On the higher edge of the land above the bowl, a few guys were setting up musical instruments under an open tent-like structure. Apparently, the games this year were going to be played with background music.

Entering The Jugg, Denney realized that she was not the only one who had recognized its convenience to the Mudbowl. Every seat at the counter was full, and Pete was fully occupied as the counterman. Denney glanced across the room to see if she knew anybody who had an extra seat at their table. "Denney, come join us!" Ana called.

Startled to see that she had overlooked Bill, Ana and Jack sitting at a table almost under her nose, she grinned at them. Ana and Bill laughed as Jack kidded her on not being able to see what was right in front of her face. "Maybe I need to arrange an eye exam for you?"

Annoyed that Ana and Bill were laughing at Jack's lame joke as if it was the funniest thing they had ever heard, Denney was about to refuse the empty chair at their table and just leave when Ana grabbed her arm and pulled her towards the seat. "Come on, we're killing time until the Mudbowl begins. Have you had breakfast?"

"No, but I'm not really hungry. I was, uh, just looking for Kellie," she said, peering around The Jugg hoping to use Kellie as an excuse to avoid sitting down.

"She's around here someplace." Ana waved her hand randomly around the room.

"Over there, at that end table in the back. Looks like she's taking an order from Professor Willoughby and Mrs. Henderson," Bill said, pointing towards Kellie, who was posed with an order pad and pen in her hand.

Not particularly wanting to make small talk with Willoughby or Henderson, Denney gave up the idea of using Kellie as a ruse and slid into the empty chair. "Maybe I will order something," she said as she picked up a menu that was stuck in a holder in the center of the table.

"Might as well, we have almost forty-five minutes until Mudbowl activities begin," Bill said after consulting the wall clock. Turning in response to Bill's comment, she was surprised at how disheveled and in need of a shave he looked. Because he still was wearing exactly what he had worn to the rally, she doubted that he had ever made it to bed. Confused, she was only half listening to whatever Jack was saying when it dawned on her that he was talking to her and she needed to listen more carefully in anticipation of sparring with him. Denney turned her attention to him and realized that except for having taken off his white coat, he also was wearing last night's clothing. Apparently, Jack and Bill both had pulled all-nighters.

Totally perplexed, she looked for guidance to Ana, but she seemed oblivious to anything being out of the ordinary. In fact, Ana was having a perfectly lovely time at breakfast. Frustrated, Denney stared at her menu as if trying to make a major decision.

"Coffee?" Kellie asked, standing over her shoulder.

"Sure," Denney replied.

"Didn't expect to see you this morning," Kellie said, as she placed a mug in front of Denney and filled it from

a steaming handheld pot. She went around the table re-
filling everybody's cups. "You're going to need to drink
a lot more of that to catch up to these three. They opened
the place."

"No," Ana corrected as she added cream to her coffee.
"Pete and you did that. We were just your first custom-
ers," she said as Denney gave Kellie her order for two
eggs over easy and an order of toast.

"What were you all doing here so early?" Denney
asked. "You," taking in the dark circles under Ana's eyes,
"look like you never went to sleep."

"Oh, I got a couple of hours when you and I got home.
Now these guys…" She stopped in mid-sentence as she
caught Bill putting his finger over his mouth as if to hush
her. "Let's just say we had things to do."

"That's right," Jack said. "We had things to do, but
we'll catch up on our sleep later today."

Seeing them grinning like three Cheshire cats, Denney began to say something and then paused as a different thought crossed her mind. "You—"

"You have good friends," Bill interrupted. "Tuesday
night, they poetically waxed that although you had prom-
ises to keep, a friend of yours here," he said, nodding
towards Jack, "ruined the part about miles to go before
you sleep. This one," he said, screwing his face up to
look pitiful while dramatically rubbing the arm nearest
Ana, "is particularly convincing. She made me see that
because you normally are a person who does what she
says she is going to do, a few of us had an obligation to
finish what you had started."

"You didn't," Denney began.

"Oh yes we did. After Ana got done with me," he
chuckled as she gave him a dirty look and missed hitting his arm by a mile, "there was no way I could help

but volunteer. After all," he said, holding up his car keys, "I have what she needed."

"We were going to take care of the problem about two o'clock this morning, but all of us were still at the rally. We never thought it would last that long," Ana explained. Lowering her voice, she continued. "Once Bill got Jack to agree to help us, they decided it would be a good idea if the two of us came to the rally with the two of you as an alibi. Our idea was that everyone would know we went to the rally and probably would see us when we got back. That way, nobody would associate us with any other campus activities. Our plan was that I would go upstairs when we got back from the rally and get Kellie. Then, the four of us, and you, if you felt up to it, would kill time until around two. The length of the concert threw a monkey wrench into everything so, instead of finishing between two and three, we were just getting started then."

"Ana stopped to wake you up," Bill offered.

"I never heard you."

"You were snoring too loudly. Seriously, you were sleeping so soundly that I figured you needed your sleep more than running around with us. It was just as well. By the time we finished, it was almost time for Kellie to go to work."

"By then, we figured it wasn't worth going to bed," Jack added. "We stopped by Bill's long enough for Kellie to clean up before going to work. After we dropped her off, we decided to have breakfast together until Mudbowl time."

"We were going to call you in a little while to meet us at the Mudbowl, and to make sure you didn't stand on the downwind side of the bowl," Ana said.

"You didn't!" Denney said in a loud voice. They all

hushed her, but just the idea of the different things that must have gone on since she said good-night to them after the rally made her start laughing to a point that she had tears in her eyes. The mental picture of the four pranksters was just too much. Grabbing a napkin from the black plastic holder, she dabbed at her eyes. "Where did you get the stuff?"

"One of Aunt Maisie's friends keeps a few horses in Chelsea. He offered us as much as we wanted for a morning's worth of mucking out the stable. We did it Wednesday morning."

"But Ana, you came up to see me. You were going to a breakfast meeting off campus."

"I only visited you for a few minutes," Ana pointed out. "Bill was waiting downstairs for me while I dropped your things off. Then, we went back to pick up Kellie, after she got off work. I didn't lie to you. We had breakfast off campus before we picked up our Mudbowl gold."

"Today is Saturday. From Wednesday to this morning, what did you do with you know what?"

"We put it in the silver freezer at Sorosis."

"You what?" Denney said.

"Shh," Jack advised, looking around to see if anyone was listening.

"We brought the dung back to Sorosis in some of the old ice cream containers that were thrown out after dinner the night we took you to Health Services," Ana explained. "You remember, we had the ice cream dessert party that night because that freezer was targeted for cleaning by the busboys this weekend. When we got back from the infirmary, Bill decided to leave his car in our parking lot for the night and walk back to the Phi Delt house, so all of us came in through the back door. Seeing the empty containers stacked for garbage, the same lightbulb went off in all of our heads."

"Kellie and Ana grabbed a bunch and wiped them out," Bill interjected. "We put them in my trunk until morning. Then, we used them to pick up the dung."

"But using the house freezer?" Denney asked.

"Oh, that was a no-brainer. With the ice cream eaten and just about everything out of the freezer and nothing new going in there until after the cleaning, it just made sense to put the cartons back where there was space for them," Ana said, as if she was explaining something as elementary as the color of the sky.

"Don't look so disgusted," Ana chided Denney. "We made sure to move anything that was edible to the other freezer before we made the silver freezer into a cold storage unit."

"It ended up working out pretty well," Bill observed. "Our only problem was this morning when Jack and I were taking the containers out of the freezer. One apparently split and leaked before the stuff froze, so the freezer was a little nasty."

"But since it is being cleaned today or tomorrow, we decided instead of calling attention to ourselves, it would be easier to keep people out of the freezer today by putting up a few signs. Ana and Kellie stuck some creative signs on the freezer doors that said: "Hungry? Eat Out. It's Mudbowl Day.""

"Those signs are what got me here for breakfast this morning," Denney explained.

"See, it worked," Ana said with such an obvious sense of satisfaction that everyone began laughing again.

"What's so funny?" Kellie asked as she brought Denney's breakfast to the table.

"Nothing much," Denney said. "Only a side of my

great friends that I've never seen before." She took a gulp of coffee. "You did wash your hands before you handled my breakfast, didn't you?"

"Of course," Kellie grinned, now understanding the giddiness of the table's occupants, "but even if I didn't, it was all natural." She looked back at the table where Henderson and Willoughby sat. "Oh drat. Mrs. Henderson is waving for me again as if I'm a taxi. She and Willoughby are in a real dither about how the administration is going to handle the tenure issue now that Dr. Ferguson is gone. Of course, I didn't help things when I told them that he already had drafted his recommendation."

Pete pointedly looked their way, and Kellie hurried to see what Mrs. Henderson needed. Bill concentrated his gaze on her back as he mused: "Ferguson submitted his recommendation?"

Denney put down her cup. "No, Kellie says he drafted it and gave it to her to type, but she can't find it. I'm just not sure what to believe." Before Bill could continue the conversation, she asked Jack a question about the status of the Phi Delt house.

While the others sipped their coffee and Denney ate her breakfast, Jack explained that the firemen and police had finished with the house and had begun permitting students, under supervision, to see if there was anything they could salvage from the ashes. According to Jack, without Ferguson as a faculty advisor to oversee everything, the national fraternity and university officials had asked Willoughby to agree to step in temporarily as the faculty representative. As far as Jack knew, most everybody had recovered whatever they could from the house. Now, it was just going to be a matter of time and dickering with insurance adjusters before it would be decided if

the structure of the house could be repaired or if it would
have to be torn down and rebuilt.

The restaurant began to empty out as students started
to wander over to the Mudbowl. Taking a last sip of her
coffee, Denney saw Mrs. Henderson and Willoughby
walking towards their table on their way to the cashier.
As they passed, Denney and Bill each gave them a big
hello. Willoughby nodded and said hello without actually stopping, but Mrs. Henderson stared through them as
she marched towards the cashier, her color-coordinated
scarf tucked neatly against her chest.

"That was rude," Denney observed, watching Willoughby handing Kellie money to pay the tab. Kellie returned to their table after taking Willoughby's money at
the cash register.

Denney nodded at Willoughby and Henderson as they
left the restaurant. "Are they seeing each other?"

"Oh no," Bill said, "they're just working on a lot
of things together both in the English department and
through their Phi Delt related activities."

"You sound pretty sure of yourself."

"Always," Bill said congenially. "Did you get them
happy again?"

"Far from it," Kellie responded. "They had no idea that
Dr. Ferguson already had made his tenure decisions. I
think I opened a can of worms when I told them."

"You've seen the tenure decisions?" Bill asked, not revealing what Denney had said earlier. Denney sat quietly,
pretending to listen to the continuing Phi Delt conversation that Jack, Ana and Bill were having.

"Dr. Ferguson gave me his draft to type. I never read
his recommendations. Until yesterday, with the confusion of the past few days, I actually forgot I had them.

Now, I can't find the folder. But even if I could, I guess his suggestions won't count for much now."

"You never know," Bill observed. He twisted his body in his chair so he could see her face more clearly. "How did you come to have the recommendations?"

"That is the $64,000 question. I've typed a number of personal things for him. Bill, you know how he worked. I'm sure Mrs. Henderson did the same for him, too, during the years she was seeing him." Bill nodded as if he fully understood and accepted what she saying.

"She what?" Denney interrupted, forgetting that she was not a part of this conversation. "I thought she was his student and then the student assistant of that other professor who worked on the Middle English Dictionary. You know, the one who died before Willoughby was brought to Michigan."

"Mrs. Henderson was, but Dr. Ferguson also had a fling with her when she was an undergraduate student," Bill volunteered. "The irony is that while he was helping her with tuition, the student assistant job in his department, and other niceties, he also was telling her he couldn't possibly leave Aunt Maisie."

"Sounds like a pattern." Kellie put their checks on the table near Bill. She picked up Denney's now empty coffee cup and stacked it on some of the other dishes she took from the table.

Bill continued. "After Mrs. Henderson graduated, she hoped that he would divorce Aunt Maisie for her. She managed to get him to put her on permanent faculty based upon her expertise, but in that environment their relationship was different. She tried to chase him a little longer, but seeing how fickle he was, she finally understood she had no future with him. She rebounded by marrying a law student named Henderson, but their marriage only lasted a few months. It was during the time she was married that Ferguson divorced Aunt Maisie."

"So, you might say, he done them both wrong," Jack said with a Western drawl. Denney jumped. She had not realized that the entire table had stopped talking and was listening to Bill's story.

"It doesn't sound like a pretty picture," Ana observed.

"It wasn't," Bill said.

"This place is beginning to empty out," Denney said. She tried to catch Kellie's eye, but Kellie had her back to them as she was clearing dirty dishes onto a tray perched on a stand. Picking up the tray, she carried it towards the kitchen as Denney noted, "We better get going or we're going to miss the impact of your efforts."

With a scraping of their chair legs, the four stood and took their respective bills to the counter to pay. As they lined up in front of the register, Kellie emerged from the kitchen to assume the cashier duties, but reaching the cash register first, Pete waved her off.

As he counted their money and made change, he made a pretense of looking out over the almost empty restaurant. "Doesn't look too busy," he grumbled. "I'd be a fool to keep much help here until the lunchtime crowd starts coming in. You opened up today," he said to Kellie, who was a few feet away wiping crumbs from the counter. "Why don't you go join these folks and watch the Mudbowl?"

Surprised, Kellie didn't move. "Come on now, go on. On me." Kellie gave him a big hug. Pete looked embarrassed. "Make sure you're back for lunchtime," he grumbled. "Try to bring some people with you."

"Yes, sir," she said as she whipped off her apron and joined her friends as they left The Jugg.

# THIRTY-EIGHT

*Saturday, December 11, 1971*

THE MUDBOWL AREA was packed. Music blared as Phi
Delts and SAEs glared at each other in mock anger before
their football game. Thetas and Tri Delts pranced around
looking cute as observers staked out the best positions
to see them get down and dirty when they got into the
mud. Trying to avoid the loud music and stay upwind,
the five walked around the edge of the Mudbowl to its
far side. As they walked, they splintered off talking to
other students and faculty members they knew. Denney
stopped for a moment to say hello to Marta and some of
the Blagdon folks, while Ana walked over to where Dr.
Harris was standing near Professor Godbolt.

For not being a sanctioned activity, there was a pretty
good turnout. Even some of the school deans and President Fleming were present. From the corner of her eye,
Denney saw Bill and Jack go over to talk to them. Watching them greet Bill, she realized that he had been telling
the truth that day after class when he told Kellie and her
he had a meeting with the Dean and President Fleming.
Obviously, there still was a lot about his involvement
with the University and his Rocklin connection that he
had yet to share with her.

The first squeals of Mudbowl delight or disgust
could be heard as the girls' tug-of-war began. Denney
was amused to see that Sorosis had managed to have

representation in the tug-of-war as Marilyn somehow had been placed on the Tri Delt team. How ironic that through Marilyn, of all people, tradition had not died. Seeing Marilyn's look of anger as she slipped and fell into the goo, Denney felt that it couldn't have happened to a nicer person.

In just a few minutes, the women were finished and the great warring football players began their game. Denney was intently watching them when a sputtering Marilyn came up and accosted her from behind. "How could you, Denney? How could you?"

"How could I what?" she asked, looking from a furious Marilyn to Brian, who stood behind her looking like an overgrown puppy. "How could I what?" she repeated.

"Manure. You did it. You put horse shit in the Mudbowl. I smelled it the minute I fell. So did all the other girls. Now, I'm going to have to miss part of the fun to go home and take a shower."

"Marilyn, think for a moment. I was in the infirmary, then the Phi Delt house burned, and last night I was at the Sinclair rally, which didn't end until early this morning. When I got back to the house, I went right to bed and didn't get up until an hour or two ago when I went for breakfast. When would I have had a chance to put anything in the Mudbowl?"

"You said you were going to do it. I heard you in the kitchen last week."

"Marilyn, you heard us talking about things that would be fun to do, but read my lips, I did not put manure or any other foreign substance into the Mudbowl. Do you understand?"

"Well, if you didn't," she sputtered, "who did?"

"I have no idea, and I really don't care," Denney said. "You're probably just imagining things, but it wasn't me.

You know, even if somebody did lace the bowl, look how big a ditch it is," she indicated its expanse with her hand. Involuntarily, Brian and Marilyn turned to look at the bowl. "Tell me, how do you think somebody knew exactly where to put manure in that huge ditch so you could be the one to fall into it? Think they brought it in last night by the truckload?"

"I don't know how you did it, but I know you did," Marilyn ranted.

"Marilyn, for the last time, I didn't do anything. Let me assure you that if I find out that somebody actually did do something, I'll let you know. But for now, you're keeping me from watching the game." Before Marilyn could respond again, Brian, looking absolutely torn between his beloved Phi Delts and Marilyn, gently took her arm and guided her away from Denney. Although still obviously upset, she allowed herself to be led away.

Seeing Ana now standing with Jack, Denney went over and told them what had just transpired with Marilyn. "If she only knew for sure, we would be dead meat," Ana said, unable to avoid taking a peak in Marilyn's direction. "Boy is she angry. Are those her parents she is standing with?"

"Probably, they come up for every game and remember, they have a special feeling for the Mudbowl." Denney turned slightly so she could see who Marilyn was standing with. "That's them. Her dad is talking to Brian. Maybe we're seeing the next generation plan a marriage at the Mudbowl."

"Now, that would be romantic," Ana said dreamily. "Imagine her telling her children that their wonderful father, Brian, asked for her hand, even knowing it had just been smeared in manure in the Mudbowl."

"Ana!" Denney hooted. "You're supposed to be the

nice one of us. Don't look now, but Marilyn is pointing us
out to Sergeant Rutledge. He must be on Mudbowl duty."
Of course, once admonished not to look the other two
immediately took furtive peeks at Marilyn and Sergeant
Rutledge. As usual, he did not look amused. "Maybe we
should divide up a little and make ourselves scarce. You
know how much he likes me."

"You two go," Ana said. "I promised Bill I would wait
here until he gets back."

"Where did he go?" Denney asked, not even realizing
that he was gone.

"Professor Willoughby wanted to show him something over at the Phi Delt house. Apparently, Mrs. Henderson and he found a book or album that the fire spared
that they think may have a connection to his father. They
wanted him to see it and thought this was a good time to
go. They won't be gone long."

"But Mrs. Henderson is over there," Jack said pointing over her shoulder towards Kellie, Dr. Harris, and
Mrs. Henderson.

"I guess only Bill and Professor Willoughby went,"
Ana said with a shrug.

Agreeing that splitting up was best, Jack strolled pur-
posely towards another group of Phi Delts. After he left,
Denney remained standing with Ana. "Did you say Bill
asked you to wait," Denney asked. Seeing Ana's face,
she wished she hadn't. Obviously, during the past few
days Ana and Bill had actually spent more time together
than she had spent with Bill. Slowly, it dawned on her
that the two had gotten to know each other fairly well
or else Ana would not have known his name at the hospital. Denney thought Ana had accompanied her to the
emergency room to keep her company, but now she understood that Ana herself had been worried about Bill.

For a moment the two stood uncomfortably looking at each other. "Den, I wanted to talk to you about what has been happening. I wouldn't do anything to hurt you. I haven't given Bill any encouragement or—"

"Ana, it's okay." As she said it, Denney knew it was. She gave Ana a quick hug. "Come on, ask Kellie. She's standing over there with Dr. Harris," Denney said, pointing behind Ana. "She'll tell you, I've always liked Bill as a friend."

Denney felt relieved at realizing why she had been so reticent about encouraging Bill. "Now," she said, "I understand why Kellie stopped pressing me to be more interested in him." Ana blushed. "I can't think of two people who belong together as a couple more than Bill and you."

"You mean that?" Ana looked relieved.

"Absolutely. Of course, now you guys have to find me somebody so we can double date."

"Jack?"

"Bite your tongue off. That guy can be so rude."

"Give him a chance. He seemed to be growing on you last night," Ana said with a big grin. "Come on, let's go rescue Kellie so she can go back to work. Mrs. Henderson and Willoughby told Godbolt and Dr. Harris that Kellie lost Dr. Ferguson's draft. Now all of them apparently are chastising her."

"Do you really believe he gave her a draft of his recommendations to type?" Denney's voice reflected her personal disbelief.

"I do. Kellie hasn't had it easy and she may stretch the truth here and there, but she basically tells it like it is. I don't know if the folder ever made it home the night Helen was killed, but if Kellie says she had a folder from Dr. Ferguson, she had it at one point that night. I'm absolutely convinced of that." Startled by Ana's vehement defense of Kellie, Denney held back as Ana started walking towards Kellie and Dr. Harris. "Are you coming?"

"No, I'm going back to the house. Maybe Kellie is telling the truth," Denney said with a funny look on her face. "I'll be back in a few minutes. In the meantime, go spring Kellie from the faculty. Looks like she is fighting off Godbolt as well as Mrs. Henderson and Dr. Harris. Besides, as human as Pete was today, Kellie better get back to work and not take advantage of him."

# THIRTY-NINE

*Saturday, December 11, 1971*

WALKING BACK TO the Sorosis house, Denney tried to think who could have gained from killing both Helen and Ferguson if the issue was tenure, but nobody came to mind. Failing to come up with a connection to the tenure issue, she tried brainstorming other possibilities. She was so involved in her own thoughts that she almost bumped into Bill and Willoughby returning from the Phi Delt house. Exchanging pleasantries, she learned that their trip had been unsuccessful. Apparently, Mrs. Henderson and Willoughby had mistaken an attendance log that Mr. Smythe had kept as house secretary as being a personal journal. She told them that Ana and everybody else still were at the Mudbowl and that she would be back as soon as she checked something at the house.

As she reached Sorosis, she paused for a moment at the edge of the brick path to admire its white sprawling form contrasted against the cloudless blue sky. It really was an inviting home. Denney refocused on her mission and continued towards the house, avoiding the places in the brick where weeds had taken the place of eroded mortar. For some reason, as she neared the building, snatches of the John Lennon song he had sung at the rally flashed through her head. She knew she was transposing lines from "Imagine," but phrases kept going through her mind along with an image of the blueness of the sky. Maybe she had inhaled too much secondhand smoke. For a moment, as she opened the unlocked door, she thought she might have the connection, but then it eluded her again.

The main floor seemed deserted. Even though Sorosis was not actually playing in the Mudbowl, except for Marilyn, the fire had created such a bonding between the Phi Delts and the Sorosis members that rather than boycotting the Mudbowl, most of the house was cheering from the sidelines.

Going straight to her room, Denney was glad she was alone. Her bed was unmade, the gray suit had possession of her chair, and the floor was strewn with the books, papers, clothing, and other things she had dropped there during the week.

Approaching the pile closest to the bed, she sat on the floor and began sorting it. She shook each piece of clothing as she threw it on a new pile to her side. As she picked up her bath towel to shake, she uncovered the folder she had used to rest the notebook on in bed yesterday. Denney picked it up and opened it. Kellie had not been lying. It contained a handwritten draft of Dr. Ferguson's recommendations.

Without moving, Denney began to read the draft. She was still in the opening sentences, when either hearing a step or realizing that the perfume scent that had clung to her suit now was almost overpowering, the blue sky image that had been nagging at her morphed in her mind into a gauzy blue scarf. She knew who was standing in the doorway behind her.

"Come in, Mrs. Henderson," she invited, before she actually turned to see her. "I think this is what you want."

"Yes, it is. I'll take that folder now," Mrs. Henderson ordered, as Denney shifted her position on the floor to face towards the door. Rolling hard to her left as an automatic reflex, Denney was just able to twist her head out of Mrs. Henderson's way as she swung Denney's hot pot at her. The blow hit Denney's right shoulder, stunning her for a moment. Before Denney could fully process how badly her shoulder was injured, Mrs. Henderson tried to hit her again. Unable to use her right arm to defend herself, Denney tried to scramble out of Mrs. Henderson's reach, but she was trapped between the bed and Mrs. Henderson.

Denney braced herself for another blow, but the jacket from Denney's gray suit came flying through the air with Kellie close behind.

The jacket, wrapping her head, blinded Henderson as the full force of Kellie's weight in a flying football tackle, knocked her into Denney. Both sprawled. Mrs. Henderson dropped the hot pot while Denney lost her grip on the folder.

With the folder on the floor, the dynamics of the fight changed. Mrs. Henderson made a lunge for it. All three of them were on the floor scrambling when Sergeant Rutledge, followed by Dr. Harris, burst into the room.

"Grab her!" Denney shouted from the floor. "No, not Kellie, grab Mrs. Henderson, before she gets away," she yelled as Sergeant Rutledge first tried to restrain a clawing Kellie while Mrs. Henderson, clutching the folder, made a break towards the door.

"Hold up there!" Officer Rutledge grunted as he gracefully changed targets and managed to body block Mrs. Henderson before she reached the doorway. With a shriek of anger and frustration, Mrs. Henderson raked her nails across his face, leaving a welt from his cheek to his chin. Sergeant Rutledge grabbed her by the arms and wrestled her to the ground. As he handcuffed a subdued Mrs.

Henderson, Kellie snatched the folder back from Mrs. Henderson's hand.

"The folder! Where did you find it?" she asked Denney, who was still sitting on the floor rubbing her aching shoulder. Without waiting for an answer, she turned on Mrs. Henderson. "That's what it was about?" she asked incredulously, holding up the folder. "Tenure?"

Mrs. Henderson did not reply.

"You killed him over tenure," Kellie repeated, as tears began running down her face.

"That was it, wasn't it?" Denney flinched as she tried to move her arm. "Dr. Ferguson figured out what you had done, so you had to kill him, too."

"No, he never figured it out." Mrs. Henderson practically spat. "He threatened me. He told me he would never give me tenure, and that he would ruin my career by insinuating my work has been less than academically sound. All the years I've put in on the dictionary would be for nothing. I couldn't let that happen," Mrs. Henderson said bitterly. "I just couldn't."

"You have a right to remain silent, Mrs. Henderson," Sergeant Rutledge said.

"I'm not going to be silent anymore! I was silent while he let me do all the work and said he loved me, but wouldn't leave his wife. I was silent while I watched him go after that little tramp." She glared at Kellie, who had gone pale.

"But why did you kill Helen?" Dr. Harris asked.

"She didn't mean to. Did you Mrs. Henderson?" Denney said.

Mrs. Henderson stared at Denney. "No, I didn't. I thought she was Suzanne. The light was dim and I—"

Dr. Harris took a deep breath, her hand finding her

throat. "You meant to kill *me*. You were going to smash my head with that bookend, like you did poor Helen...."

"You didn't have to kill anyone," Denney said quietly. "Ferguson may have said those things to you, but, you know what's ironic?" She turned to Kellie. "Read the first paragraph of his memo to the tenure committee."

Opening the folder, Kellie glanced at the top page for a moment, and then she began to read aloud: "It is with sincere regret that I am unable to comply with your instruction to identify only two candidates for tenure, because the English department has four qualified candidates who, I respectfully submit, should be granted tenure. The documented growth and strength of the English department forces me to respectfully disagree with a limitation to two names. Consequently, for the reasons given herein, I urge reconsideration of this year's policy and recommend tenure for Suzanne Harris, Brenda Henderson, Sean Willoughby and Franklin Godbolt." Reacting to a small intake of breath from Mrs. Henderson, Kellie stopped reading.

For a moment, the only sounds in the room were Kellie's quiet sniffling and Mrs. Henderson's sobs. Then, Sergeant Rutledge led Mrs. Henderson away.

# FORTY

A FEW HOURS later, Kellie, Ana, Jack, Denney and Dr. Harris were squeezed around the same round table at The Jugg that the group had claimed that morning. Jack had found Denney's shoulder to only be badly bruised, but it still ached. Bill finished talking to his dad on the pay phone and joined them. He slid into the chair next to Ana, taking her hand. Denney, sitting across from Ana and Bill, gave them a smile of encouragement, almost as warm as the one she gave Jack when he moved his chair closer to hers.

"Well," said Bill. "Dad says Sergeant Rutledge told him that it is official. You are no longer a suspect in Helen's death, Suzanne. Mrs. Henderson confessed again to killing both Helen and Dr. Ferguson. She actually set the Phi Delt fire to cover murdering Ferguson."

"She could have killed Moose, too," Jack observed. "I wonder if they will charge her with anything besides murder?"

"Possibly," Kellie said. "What I don't understand is that as cruel as Dr. Ferguson could be, what made Mrs. Henderson snap at the fraternity house instead of in his office or somewhere where there would have been less people?"

"Apparently, she went back to the Phi Delt house that morning to meet Ferguson to finalize some of the Mudbowl activities," Bill said. "She must have just missed your brother, Kellie, because when she got there Dr. Ferguson already was in a confrontational mood. That's when they got into it about the tenure issue. He taunted her unmercifully and then ended the discussion by just sitting down in one of the wing chairs that make a conversation area facing the bay window. She was so furious that she grabbed one of the fire tools and bashed him in the head from behind. Petrified, she used some of the candles that had been lit during the meeting the night before to start a fire by igniting the curtains and some of the papers on the desk. She took a chance that nobody would come into the room before the fire was burning well."

"So the direction of his chair was why you didn't see Dr. Ferguson," Denney stated.

"Right. I never went any further into the room than the couch that Moose was passed out on. The chairs, facing the window, were beyond the couch. By the time I got there, that part of the meeting room already was in flames."

"But Mrs. Henderson was outside," Kellie said.

"That's right. She called Willoughby about some Mudbowl problem and then left the fraternity and got in her car to intercept him on the street so that she could have an alibi that put her outside the house. Mrs. Henderson planned to let him see her through the car window and then drive away in the confusion of the fire," Bill said.

Denney thought about how Mrs. Henderson had looked at the hospital. "If her plan had worked, nobody would have seen how disheveled she was at the beginning of the fire."

"But Willoughby didn't know her plans, and thought she was the best way to get me to the emergency room quickly. By the time she got back with Aunt Maisie, everyone attributed her not looking her usual perfect self to having transported Aunt Maisie and me."

"Maybe I'm not thinking perfectly clearly," Dr. Harris said, "but I don't understand why Mrs. Henderson thought she didn't have a shot at tenure."

Bill cradled his coffee. "It was fairly common knowledge that Suzanne's publications alone justified her getting one of the tenured spots and she felt Willoughby probably had the other spot because of something he had on Dr. Ferguson."

"What made her think that Willoughby had a stronger connection to Dr. Ferguson than she did?" Ana asked.

"According to Dad, it dates back to when Ferguson and Willoughby were active Phi Delts, and fairly good friends. Using Willoughby's car, they doubled for formals the year they were juniors. Dr. Ferguson and his date started the evening in the backseat, but when the four left the party to go to the Arboretum to watch the sun come up, Ferguson decided that Willoughby was too far gone to drive so he took the wheel. Nobody quite knows whether he fell asleep, passed out, or just ran a red light, but they crashed. Willoughby's date survived, but never regained a memory of the accident. Dr. Ferguson and Willoughby only had minor injuries, but Ferguson's date was killed.

"This is where Willoughby supposedly got his ammunition against Ferguson. The unproven version of the story is that while they were waiting for help, Ferguson knew that as much as he had had to drink, he was going to be in real trouble, so he forced Willoughby to help him pull his date from the passenger side of the car to behind the wheel, and then he went around and got into the passenger side. When help came, they both said she had been driving. As long as their story was the same, nobody could prove otherwise, but the fraternity talk was that Ferguson would never have let a woman drive.

"After the accident Ferguson overtly cleaned up his act. Most people believed the public version of the accident story, and actually felt bad for him at having lost what was now considered to have been his true love. He got a position on staff, became the faculty advisor for the Phi Delts, and then married Aunt Maisie, who was a lot younger than he was."

"But your father believed the unpublicized story," Denney surmised.

"That's right. He didn't want Aunt Maisie to marry Ferguson, but since Dad couldn't prove anything about the swap story, he couldn't say anything. The only thing he could do was keep him from being my godfather. From her student days, and having dated Dr. Ferguson, Mrs. Henderson had heard all the stories, too. She had a pretty good idea what was true and what wasn't."

Dr. Harris shook her head. "So Brenda really did think she had to get rid of me."

"She was so desperate for tenure that she felt she had to knock off her competitors. Unlike Willoughby, your academics were too strong for her to attack. Knowing you often worked alone late at night, she must have felt you were an easier target to reach physically," Bill said.

"Henderson already was upset that night by how badly Ferguson had treated her at the poetry party. When she came up the back stairs and walked by your office, she saw the perfect opportunity."

"And Denney you figured this out because of the blue scarf?" Dr. Harris mused. "I wonder if it just fell off or if they struggled and Helen grabbed it?"

"We may never know." Denney bit her lip, hoping Helen had died quickly.

"I thought it was Helen's scarf because it was lying on her neck," Bill said. "Like me, nobody ever connected it with anyone else."

"But the blue didn't go with what Helen was wearing," Denney noted. "Helen was too put together for that. It bothered me subconsciously, but I couldn't put my finger on it for a long time."

"It's all horrible," Ana said. "I don't understand why Mrs. Henderson didn't try to go after Dr. Harris again?" Bill put a comforting arm around her shoulders.

"I think Mrs. Henderson was too busy trying to eliminate Willoughby," Denney said. "She sabotaged his proof pages by changing the order of the proofs and maybe even threw out some of the pages that Helen had finished working on. From the pile of pages that the police confiscated the night Helen was killed, it looks like Helen might have figured out that something wasn't the way it should be. The stacks she was making should have been divided into A to M headings, but, the copies I tried to put in order in the elevator also contained sheets with Mrs. Henderson's alphabet letters."

"The police can't prove it," Bill said, "but they think Helen was trying to reconcile the original hard copy pages with the proofs to see what had been altered, when she decided to get a cup of tea. According to Dad," Bill continued, "what they do know for sure is that while Helen was in your office, Mrs. Henderson killed her, and then went to her own office. She buzzed Dr. Ferguson from her office to establish an alibi."

"That must have been who he went to see when he left you alone in his office, Kellie," Denney pointed out.

"In the meantime, you came up the back stairs," Bill

said, directing his remarks to Dr. Harris, "and you not only found Helen, you picked up the murder weapon. In the confusion of your screaming, Denney and me coming in, and Willoughby being so thick when we needed to call the police, nobody could remember exactly when Mrs. Henderson was in her own office. Her alibi idea worked because Ferguson told them he had been in her office just around the time the murder had taken place."

"Did she really come after you at the hospital?" Jack asked Denney.

"She did," Denney replied. "When I stopped her that night outside Angell Hall, she kept pulling her coat tighter. At the time I thought she was just cold, but now I realize she had missed her scarf and was afraid I would remember her wearing it at the poetry party, but then not having it on when she left Angell Hall. I did realize it, but not until just before she attacked me at Sorosis when the blue of the scarf and the smell of the perfume came together."

"But how did she know you were still in the infirmary?" Ana asked.

"Guilty," said Jack, hitting his head. "After I got off duty, I was supposed to meet with Dr. Ferguson at his office to confirm how Bill was going to be inducted. When I got there, Mrs. Henderson was already in his office discussing something. Irritated as I was about the last exchange you and I had had, Denney, I probably mouthed off a little about how you were complicating my Phi Delt duties with Bill."

"That clears up another mystery," Denney said. "Maybe Mrs. Henderson wasn't quite sure what she was going to do about me, but she knew the infirmary would be pretty empty at that hour. Spying the syringe Jack left for an emergency must have seemed like providence to her. It would have worked except for the scent of her perfume getting to me."

"The scent of her perfume?" Dr. Harris asked.

"As Kellie later told me, Dr. Ferguson apparently gave all of the women who worked in his department the same perfume last year. Helen wore hers regularly, and in my half-witted state of mind, I had the sensation Helen was in my room. The feeling was strong enough to rouse me, and actually saved me."

"Maybe she was there," Dr. Harris said softly. "I'd like to think so."

"I would, too."

After a long moment of silence, Denney cleared her throat. "In the meantime, I owe you an apology, Dr. Harris. Until I was sitting in my room looking at the folder with the draft recommendation, and smelled the perfume scent, I thought it was you. It was only at that moment that I realized it had to be Mrs. Henderson behind me."

"Why?" Dr. Harris asked.

"Because of a new song by John Lennon. Parts of it about unity and being one have been going around in my head all day with a surreal image of blue that I finally realized was the scarf. When I read the first sentence where Dr. Ferguson tried to recommend all four of you, I knew Helen had been killed by mistake. Without knowing that he was putting all four of you forward, the killer had to have been motivated by the need to get rid of the top candidates."

"But why did Mrs. Henderson take a chance of coming to the Sorosis house?"

"She was afraid of what the recommendation in the folder said about her. Dr. Ferguson had been pretty cruel, and her career, which he had threatened, was all she had."

"I looked when we were in your room the other day,

but never saw the folder," Kellie said. "How did you know where to find it?"

"It wasn't rocket science. When I came back from my shower and found you in my room reading the notes I had made in bed in the notebook, I got angry and threw my towel and other things on my bed. I never really looked for the folder again because I didn't believe you about it. It was only when Ana said she was going to rescue you from the faculty chastising you about losing the folder," she said, glancing at Kellie with embarrassment, "that I remembered that I had rested your notebook on a folder when I made my notes. I figured that if I had used your notebook, I probably had used your folder, too. Knowing how much I had thrown on my floor after the Sinclair rally, there was a good chance it was either there or stuck in my blankets. I'm sorry, Kel," Denney apologized. "What I haven't figured out though is why you came back to the house?"

"That's simple. Ana broke up the discussion the faculty members were having with me by announcing that you had an idea where the folder might be. After her interruption, the heat was off of me and everybody suddenly had places to be. I happened to look up and see Mrs. Henderson walking behind you. You already had reached the Sorosis walkway, but what struck me wrong was that she was way past what should have been her Washtenaw destination, the Phi Delt house. Call it woman's intuition or just reading too many mysteries, but I told Dr. Harris I was going to your room and that she needed to get Sergeant Rutledge from the other side of the Mudbowl and meet us there."

"I did as I was told. From that point, you know the rest." Dr. Harris offered a basket of fries to Denney, who took one.

"Oh yeah," Bill said in response to Ana's prodding his side, "there is one more piece of information that Denney, Ana, and my parents want to share with this group. First, my parents want you to know how appreciative they were of everyone at Sorosis helping the Phi Delts out after the fire. Also, they want you to know that when Dad was at Sorosis the night Sergeant Rutledge was interviewing us, an application was formally made to the Rocklin Foundation. That application has been approved. Kellie, you need to stop by the financial aid office next week because they have some papers for you to sign for a Rocklin Scholarship that will cover your tuition, room and board for next year."

Kellie, clearly in shock, held her hand over her mouth. "What!" She jumped up. "I can't believe it!"

After a round of hugs, Bill, holding Ana's hand again, looked across the table at Denney and asked, "Does that wrap everything up?"

Denney smiled. "For the moment."

\* \* \* \* \*

# ABOUT THE AUTHOR

Judge, award-winning author, litigator, wife, step-mom, mother of twins, civic volunteer, Yankee, and Southern Woman writer are all words used to describe Debra H. Goldstein. *Maze in Blue*, her debut novel, is a murder mystery set on a university campus.

Judge Debra H. Goldstein, a loyal University of Michigan alumna, lives in Birmingham, Alabama, with her husband, a die-hard Alabama fan.

# REQUEST YOUR FREE BOOKS!

## 2 FREE NOVELS
## PLUS 2 FREE GIFTS!

**WORLDWIDE LIBRARY**®
Your Partner in Crime

# *ReaderService*.com

## Manage your account online!

- Review your order history
- Manage your payments
- Update your address

*We've designed
the Harlequin® Reader Service
website just for you.*

## Enjoy all the features!

- Reader excerpts from any series
- Respond to mailings and
  special monthly offers
- Discover new series available to you
- Browse the Bonus Bucks catalog
- Share your feedback

*Visit us at:*
## ReaderService.com

RS13